What Others Are Saying
about R.J. Patterson

"R.J. Patterson does a fantastic job at keeping you engaged and interested. I look forward to more from this talented author."

- Aaron Patterson
bestselling author of SWEET DREAMS

DEAD SHOT

"Small town life in southern Idaho might seem quaint and idyllic to some. But when local newspaper reporter Cal Murphy begins to un-cover a series of strange deaths that are linked to a sticky spider web of deception, the lid on the peaceful town is blown wide open. Told with all the energy and bravado of an old pro, first-timer R.J. Patterson hits one out of the park his first time at bat with *Dead Shot*. It's that good."

- Vincent Zandri
bestselling author of THE REMAINS

"You can tell R.J. knows what it's like to live in the newspaper world, but with *Dead Shot*, he's proven that he also can write one heck of a murder mystery."

- Josh Katzowitz
NFL writer for CBSSports.com
& author of Sid Gillman: Father of the Passing Game

"Patterson has a mean streak about a mile wide and puts his two main characters through quite a horrible ride, which makes for good reading."

- Richard D., reader

DEAD LINE

"This book kept me on the edge of my seat the whole time. I didn't really want to put it down. R.J. Patterson has hooked me. I'll be back for more."

- Bob Behler
-time Idaho broadcaster of the year
v-play voice for Boise State football

"Like a John Grisham novel, from the very start I was pulled right into the story and couldn't put the book down. It was as if I personally knew and cared about what happened to each of the main characters. Every chapter ended with so much excitement and suspense I had to continue to read until I learned how it ended, even though it kept me up until 3:00 A.M.

- Ray F., reader

DEAD IN THE WATER

"In Dead in the Water, R.J. Patterson accurately captures the action-packed saga of a what could be a real-life college football scandal. The sordid details will leave readers flipping through the pages as fast as a hurry-up offense."

- Mark Schlabach,
ESPN college sports columnist and
co-author of *Called to Coach*
and *Heisman: The Man Behind the Trophy*

THE WARREN OMISSIONS

"What can be more fascinating than a super high concept novel that reopens the conspiracy behind the JFK assassination while the threat of a global world war rests in the balance? With his new novel, *The Warren Omissions*, former journalist turned bestselling author R.J. Patterson proves he just might be the next worthy successor to Vince Flynn."

- Vincent Zandri
bestselling author of THE REMAINS

HARD

TARGET

A Brady Hawk novel

R.J.
PATTERSON

Hard Target
© Copyright 2017 R.J. Patterson

First Print Edition 2017

Cover Design by Books Covered

Published in the United States of America
Green E-Books
Boise Idaho 83713

For Stella, who kept me sane in an insane newsroom

CHAPTER 1

Port Said, Egypt

BRADY HAWK SCANNED THE DOCKS in search of *Hamamat Alsalam*, an aging fishing boat that housed his target. A flock of seagulls circled overhead and squawked, ruining an otherwise peaceful evening. As the last few moments of daylight flickered across the rippling water, Hawk checked his watch and then continued to look for any activity in the harbor. The picture in his pocket showed several distinct features of the *Hamamat Alsalam*, but the vessels moored below his location all looked like they had seen better days with fading paint jobs and rusting hulls common-place. With the boats packed in tightly, Hawk struggled to identify the one he planned to board.

After a half hour of searching, Hawk grew tired of the rote chore and had almost decided to ditch his binoculars and venture closer when he spotted movement on one of the ship's decks. An armed guard roamed around the ship, pausing every few feet to stoop over the railing and look at the docks. The appearance of any type of patrol was unusual on its own, but a man with a weapon was a dead giveaway.

Amateurs.

Hawk studied the ship closely for a few more seconds in an attempt to read the name painted on the back. In the dim light, he caught the word Hamamat, which was enough to convince him that was his target. He stuffed his gear into his tactical bag, slung it over his shoulder, and headed straight for the *Hamamat Alsalam.*

"I found her," Hawk said over his com.

"About time," Alex Duncan answered from the safety of an apartment in Washington, D.C.

"I'm never good enough for you, am I?"

"I can't let you get the big head, now can I?"

Hawk chuckled to himself but didn't say a word as he passed a pair of men strolling along the docks.

"What's the matter? You don't have a witty comeback for me this time?"

"Time to go to work, Alex."

Hawk scanned the deck of the *Hamamat Alsalam* for any more soldiers milling around. From his position, he couldn't see anyone. He crept closer to the ship before stealthily climbing the ladder attached to the side. Once Hawk reached the top, he spotted a guard asleep on top of a large crate. Not wanting to take any chances, Hawk pistol whipped the guard in the head, ensuring he remained unconscious while Hawk did his job.

The seagulls dispersed and a cool breeze eased across the deck, carrying the waft of salt water. The only sounds were the lapping of water against boat hulls and the occasional roar of an offshore wave.

Hawk would've preferred to be walking hand-in-hand with Alex on a nearby beach instead of heading into a den of terrorists. But the men hidden away in the ship held no regard for Hawk's wishes—or anyone else's, for that matter. Their mission consisted of utilizing fear as leverage to get what they wanted, though their end game seemed rather hazy to Hawk. Revenge? Annihilation of America? World domination? To the rational mind, Hawk thought each possible objective was juvenile or overly idealistic. But these weren't rational men—and Hawk knew that fact all too well. They couldn't be appeased or negotiated with. No cost was too high to achieve whatever it was they held as their goal. Far too often, Hawk concluded that Al Hasib was only interested in the act of terrorizing, devoid of any true purpose. And Hawk was going to snuff them out as long as he could until they either submitted or were rendered toothless.

"How many heat signatures do you see?" Hawk asked Alex.

"I can see three, including the man you just knocked out. Should be easy enough now with just two guards below, but then again, this is Brady Hawk we're talking about."

"Are you saying I make things difficult on purpose?"

"I do recall you acting against my advice, oh, I don't know—several dozen times."

"But I'm still standing."

"Maybe you could give my ticker a break and just handle this op straightforward for once, okay?"

Hawk smiled as he stole below. "One simple op coming right up."

Once Hawk reached the lower deck, he peered around the corner and saw a pair of guards talking softly over a game of cards. The men were arguing over who was scheduled to make the rounds once their companion returned. One of the guards suggested they play for it instead.

How about both of you take the night off?

Hawk fired two shots from across the room, the first one hitting the guard on the right in the head, the second drilling the other soldier in the chest. The first man died instantly, but the second struggled after he fell out of his chair and tried to reach his gun. Hawk used two more bullets to squash the man's hope.

"Simple enough for you?" Hawk chided.

"Are they all dead?" Alex asked.

"All except for the guy up top, but he's going to be asleep for a long time."

"Consider me satisfied then. Now all you need to do is find the weapons system."

Hawk scanned the room, which was relatively empty save a few wooden crates in the corner. Rushing over to them, he tried to pry off the lids. But they weren't budging. Hawk looked around the room for something to help give him leverage until he found a long wooden paddle.

"This should do the trick," Hawk said.

"Do the trick? Are you having problems?" Alex asked.

"Let's just say things could be going better, but I'm making progress now."

Jamming the oar in a small gap between the lid and the box, Hawk worked to loosen the top. After a few moments, the wood creaked as the nails broke free. Hawk wasted no time, immediately reaching inside to put his hands on and verify he'd located the device. Without finding anything but packing straw, he plunged his hands deeper inside.

Nothing.

"It's not here," Hawk said.

"Forget that," Alex said. "You've got company."

"What?"

"Two more heat signatures moving along the corridor toward your position."

Hawk raced over to the doorway and braced for a fight. When the first guard rushed inside the room, Hawk broadsided him, taking the man to the floor before putting two bullets in his chest. When Hawk was finished, he looked up and found exactly what he expected—another guard who was taken aback by the violent nature of Hawk's attack. Hawk rolled onto his back, pulling the dead body with him to use as a shield.

The guard at the door trained his weapon on Hawk, but he slung a knife at the guard's arm, forcing him to drop his gun. Hawk shoved the body off and scrambled to his feet. The guard screamed with pain as he stared at the knife.

Hawk grabbed the knife and yanked it out of the man's arm, resulting in further screams.

"First time in combat?" Hawk asked in Arabic.

The man nodded.

Hawk guessed the man couldn't have been any older than twenty.

"Now, I'm looking for something on this boat, and I am hoping you can help me find it," Hawk said, forcing the man across the room. "Have you seen any other large crates?"

The guard shook his head.

"Hawk," Alex squawked, "it's in the room."

"What is?" Hawk asked.

"The tracking signal is coming from the corner of the room where you're at."

"Are you sure?"

"GPS coordinates don't lie," she said.

"Fine," Hawk said before he picked up a rope and bound the man's hands. Hawk tied him to a chair and wrapped twine around the man and the chair, securing them both to a pole in the middle of the room.

"That ought to hold him," Hawk said. "Now, where exactly are we looking?"

"In the north corner of the room," Alex said.

Hawk strode toward the stack of boxes where he'd searched earlier to no avail. Sifting through the straw, he felt for the large object that wasn't to be found.

"There's nothing here," Hawk said. "And by that, I mean *nothing*. No hardware, no weapons, no anything."

"It's got to be there," she said. "The tracker is still transmitting from your location. I know these coordinates can be off by several feet, but based on what I'm seeing, you appear to be standing over it."

Hawk stormed across the room to the guard and spoke to him in Arabic. "Where is the weapon?"

"I don't know what you're talking about."

Hawk punched the man in the gut and glared as he regained his composure.

"I'll ask you again. Where is the weapon?"

"What weapon?"

Hawk recoiled and unleashed a vicious kick with his boot heel on the man's knee. The guard screamed in pain.

"Where is the weapon?"

"Stop," the man cried. "I'll tell you what you want to know."

Hawk stepped back and waited for a moment.

Looking up at Hawk, the guard winced as he spoke. "There are no weapons on this ship."

"That's not what my tracking system says," Hawk said as he narrowed his eyes and knelt down to get eye level with his prisoner. "It says there's a weapon right here in this room."

"Your machine is mistaken. There isn't one."

Unsatisfied with the man's answer, Hawk hustled back to the corner of the room and searched the box again. Determined the prove either Alex or the Al Hasib guard right, he ripped through the straw until he heard what sounded like some object bouncing on the floor and sliding.

What was that?

Hawk spun around and scanned the floor for the culprit. That's when he noticed a small electronic device with a flashing red light.

"Alex," Hawk said. "I think I found it, but you're not gonna believe this."

"Try me."

"Fazil or one of his thugs figured out a way to remove the tracking system and keep it active," he said.

"I thought it wasn't supposed to work if the device was tampered with."

"Apparently there's a workaround—and someone figured it out."

"So, now what?"

"Fortunately, I have a prisoner, so perhaps I can persuade him to tell me where it's at," Hawk said. "I'm going to hang up now because you won't want to hear this."

He switched his com off despite Alex's pleas to reconsider.

"I told you the weapon wasn't here," the guard said in English.

"Oh, so you speak English? That should make it easier for me to communicate. My Arabic is limited to phrases like, 'I'm going to shoot you in the head' or 'How do you like walking?'"

"There's nothing more to say," the guard said, struggling with his ropes. "There is no weapon on this ship."

Hawk eyed the guard cautiously. "But there *was*, wasn't there?"

"I don't know for sure, but I was told to have you call someone if I ever got into this situation."

"And who would that be?"

"Karif Fazil."

Hawk smiled. "I'd love the opportunity to speak with him. Let me get you the phone."

Hawk reached into the man's pocket and fished out his phone.

"Why don't you go ahead and give me that number now?" Hawk asked.

"I can't," the man said. "It doesn't work like that. I need to call him first."

"Why? To save face?"

"Please, just let me dial the number myself."

Hawk shook his head. "Not going to happen. Now, you give me the number or I'm going to make you forget about your left knee because I'm going to curb stomp your right knee."

"Okay, okay. He won't like it, but here it is," the man said before proceeding to reel off a string of numbers.

Hawk dialed Fazil and waited as the phone rang. After the third ring, a voice Hawk knew all too well answered the phone.

"Is it finished?" Fazil asked in Arabic.

"Depends on what you thought the job was," Hawk answered.

"Ah, Mr. Hawk," Fazil said. "I see you've managed to locate one of my transport boats."

"That's not what I was looking for," Hawk said.

Fazil laughed. "Always one step behind, aren't you?"

"I've got a pile of your dead men here that would disagree with that assessment."

"Those men are expendable, Mr. Hawk—just like the boat you're on."

A scream from the prisoner arrested Hawk's attention. He glanced over to see the man staring wide-eyed at something in front of him. A digital display on a box attached to a weight-bearing pole flashed numbers on the screen: 13, 12, 11 . . .

"So much for being one step ahead," Fazil said.

Hawk darted toward the stairwell, taking two or three steps at a time. Once he reached the main deck, he leapt as far as he could over the railing and into the water. He was barely submerged when he felt the vibrations from the blast. Swimming deeper into the murky water of Port Said, Hawk remained beneath the surface for over a minute.

When he finally came up for air, Hawk watched as flames engulfed the ship and dock personnel worked to put out the fire in an effort to keep it from spreading to one of the other nearby ships. He shook his head at the situation. His mission had failed to recover the weapons system. It was never onboard in the first place.

As Hawk hoisted himself onto the dock, he mulled over the state of affairs. He couldn't deny that Fazil was one step and knew turning the table on the Al Hasib leader wouldn't be easy.

But getting played for a fool—and nearly dying in the process—only made Hawk that more resolute. Whatever Fazil was planning, Hawk decided he would do anything necessary to stop it.

Anything.

CHAPTER 2

J.D. BLUNT HELD THE FISHING LINE between his teeth and bit down hard before yanking at the string. With the choppy waters of the Eastern Bay tossing the boat back and forth, he clamped down harder. After several tugs, the twine severed, leaving Blunt with a tight knot on his lure and a satisfied smile on his face. He studied the bait before casting it at least thirty meters off the side of the boat.

"Another fine toss, J.D.," Thomas Colton said. The CEO of Colton Industries, the country's premier weapons manufacturer, cracked open a beer and leaned back in his seat.

"That's not the only bait he likes to set," General Van Fortner quipped.

Fortner, who'd just been reassigned to the Pentagon by acting President Noah Young, flung his line out onto the water as well, outdistancing Blunt by several meters.

"Now you're just showing off," Blunt said.

"You two are both impressive when it comes to slinging line into the water, but neither of you have been able to catch anything," Colton said.

"It's because of all this damn noise on the boat," Blunt said with a growl. "If you'd sit your ass down for a minute instead of stomping all over and yelling at us like we're trying to have a conversation at a rock concert, maybe the fish would hang around for a few minutes and nibble on these spinners."

"Someone didn't take his laxative this morning," Colton said.

"I swear, I'm gonna drive this boat offshore and feed you to some sharks if you don't shut up," Blunt said.

"Well, we aren't just here to fish," Fortner said. "There are some more pressing matters that we all need to discuss sooner rather than later."

Blunt didn't say a word, keeping his eyes fixated on his line still hanging limp from the end of his rod. Patiently, he reeled in his spinner, waiting for his line to tighten so he could set the hook. Once he finished, he stood and stared out over the water. He watched with a mixture of disgust and anger as a large bass swam beneath the boat.

"Did you see that?" Blunt asked as he pointed at the water.

"I thought we were supposed to be quiet," Colton said. "I never can keep up with these whimsical rules."

"That sucker was huge," Blunt said.

Fortner leaned over the railing to look and shrugged. "Guess it's gone now."

A buzzing noise in the distance grew louder. Blunt scanned the horizon and noticed an inflatable raft powered by an outboard motor chugging straight toward them.

"I can promise it's gone for good now," Blunt said. "Doesn't anyone know about the importance of remaining as quiet as possible while you're on the water fishing? Doesn't anyone know how well sound travels through water?"

"We came here to talk," Colton said. "At least, I did. I would've never agreed to come out here just to fish, that much is certain."

The raft eased up next to their boat. A man stood and waved before tossing a rope to Fortner.

"Mind giving us a hand?" the boat's apparent captain asked.

Recognizing the U.S. Coast Guard markings on the small watercraft, Fortner tied off the rope to Blunt's ship and held out his hand. Instead of the captain climbing aboard, his two passengers stepped forward: Alex Duncan and Brady Hawk.

The captain gestured for Fortner to disentangle the two vessels. He complied and used an oar to shove away the small boat to a safe distance.

"Hawk, I can't decide who likes to torture me more—you or Mr. Colton here?" Blunt said.

"The fish aren't biting, are they?" Alex asked as a wry grin spread across her face.

"Is it that obvious?" Blunt said as he hung his head.

"Usually, I get a greeting somewhat warmer than that," she said.

Blunt narrowed his eyes and stared out across the water. "Just be glad that today I didn't shoot at you."

"That bad, huh?" Hawk asked.

"Not even a nibble," Blunt said, shaking his head.

"Bad day fishing beats a good working, eh?" Colton said.

Blunt huffed a soft laugh through his nose. "If only this day was just about fishing. Since that's obviously not going to happen, we might as well discuss what we're all here to talk about."

Blunt ushered everyone below deck and into the modest cabin. It had seating for eight, which was plenty of room for the group assembled.

Once they were all seated, Fortner opened the conversation.

"There's quite a concern in the intelligence community, especially at the Pentagon, about what Karif Fazil might do with the weapons system he stole from Colton Industries. There have been numerous theories floated around, but I wanted us all to discuss this collectively and see if we can reach a conclusion on what he might be planning."

Hawk raised his hand. "Before we get into that, can I make a polite suggestion that all Colton Industries weapons include a more undetectable tracker in the event of another heist? I was just sent on a wild goose chase that almost got me killed."

"I know it might be of little consolation to you now," Colton began, "but our engineers are already working on it."

"That's a start," Hawk said.

"Well, regarding the matter at hand," Blunt said, "I'm not sure I've got any better ideas on where Al Hasib might be planning to target. Quite frankly, there isn't a spot that's better than another."

"J.D., have you spoken with Justin Frazier at the NSA?" Fortner asked.

"I gave him a call, and we discussed what was happening," Blunt said of the NSA chief. "But if he knows anything more than what's out there in the intelligence community, he wasn't saying. I've known Frazier a long time, and based on his demeanor, I'd say he's in the dark like the rest of us."

"Does anyone think Fazil is planning on targeting any U.S. harbors?" Colton asked.

"I wouldn't rule anything out," Fortner said. "That would be a risky proposition, but Al Hasib has never operated under any type of conventional strategy. Their end game appears to be terror, in and of itself."

"Based on some of the chatter I've been monitoring, I think I know Al Hasib's target with this weapon," Alex said.

Fortner's eyebrows shot upward. "You've heard something we haven't?"

She nodded. "The Strait of Hormuz."

"Oh my God," Colton said. "That's the nightmare scenario."

Fortner nodded. "Yeah, you're not kidding. Seventeen million barrels of oil pass through there everyday, roughly thirty-five percent of all seaborne oil. It'd be an epic crisis without an end in sight."

Blunt looked at Alex. "Do you really think Iran is going to be okay with this? They've been threatening to do this for years but have never made good on it."

"From what I've gathered from my sources, Al Hasib is working in conjunction with Iran," Alex said. "The Iranians are permitting this under the table so they can be the heroes and amass some leverage on the international community when they shut it down."

"Everyone will see right through it," Fortner said.

Alex shrugged. "Maybe, but will anyone really care once gas prices sky rocket? Those leading nations will just want to reestablish stability in the region. They won't care what it cost."

"Well, that's one theory," Colton said. "Got any—"

"This isn't just a theory," Alex said. "My sources are solid on this one. And from what I understand, they could have the weapons system in place and operational in less than a week."

"We're going to need something actionable before we start an international incident," Fortner said. "Iran isn't going to take too kindly to any kind of intervention by Americans, even if it is off the book."

"What else do you need to know?" Hawk asked. "If Alex says it's solid, you can bank on that."

"We need to verify that's where the weapon is, preferably by some high-ranking officer in Al Hasib."

"What about the highest ranking officer?" Blunt asked.

"Karif Fazil?" Fortner asked. "If we can kill two birds with one stone here, I'd tell you to do just about anything. Fazil's head would be a nice trophy, not to mention it'd help Noah Young's chances at winning the presidency."

"That seems rather ambitious," Hawk said. "I'm not sure we'd be able to pull that off so quickly, especially given the time crunch we're facing. Supposing Alex is right, as soon as this weapon goes live in the Strait of Hormuz, things are going to get ugly. And our degree of difficulty increases significantly."

"Look, I get what you're saying, Hawk," Fortner began, "but as troubling as an incident as this could become, venturing into Iran's domain to eliminate a threat that they might be welcoming for various political reasons will put our country in a difficult predicament. Besides, this potential threat by Al Hasib is wreaking havoc with the financial market, not about killing people."

"That shouldn't detract from the urgency in this case," Hawk said. "We don't know what Al Hasib could be planning next. This could just be the first domino to fall in their plans."

"Plans we can only speculate about," Colton chimed in.

"Enough, Tom," Blunt said. "We know you're just hoping this whole thing blows over because you're going to get raked over the coals if it comes out that your faulty security measures allowed this to happen."

"So, what? The general is still right. We need to verify before we storm in there and ruffle a bunch of feathers in the Middle East. Isn't that the whole reason this team exists?"

"It is," Hawk said. "We're supposed to be doing things behind the scenes to avoid any big international incidents. It's why time is of the essence if we're going to keep this situation from ever escalating to that point."

"I think we can do both," Alex said.

"Get verification and prevent this from happening?" Hawk asked. "You know something I don't?"

Alex winked at Hawk. "Of course I do. How do you feel about a trip to Cuba?"

"Guantanamo Bay?" Fortner asked. "Do you know what kind of hoops I'd have to jump through to grant you access there?"

"I'm sure you can handle it," she said.

"And what exactly is the type of information you expect to get out of a bunch of incarcerated terrorists who've been there for months, if not years?" Hawk asked.

"This won't be about the kind of information we can get," she said. "It's going to be about the kind of information we can give."

Hawk studied her closely but remained quiet.

"Let's get out of here," Alex said to Blunt. "Hawk and I have a plane to catch."

CHAPTER 3

NOAH YOUNG CRACKED HIS KNUCKLES as he hovered over a report strewn across his desk. He could feel the sweat begin to bead on his forehead. Ever since President Michaels's shocking death at Camp David a week ago, Young's life had been a blur. He took center stage in the nation just two days ago, speaking at Michaels's funeral. Young had struggled to find meaningful and honest words about his predecessor, but he cobbled together a eulogy that was sufficiently comforting and heart warming while remaining truthful. Yet the forty-eight hours that separated the funeral and the present felt like a lifetime ago.

While Michaels's funeral arrangements were being organized, there was a more pressing matter to the country: How to handle the election. The opposing party vehemently opposed a lengthy delay. Their candidate, James Peterson, had ginned up their voter base and was leading by a substantial margin in the polls. Michaels's popularity had waned, but there was still strong public support for Young.

As a former war hero, Young possessed credentials that would force Peterson to answer questions which would've remained buried had Michaels been the opponent. Young flew fighter jets and served in the first Gulf War, while Peterson—Young's elder by a couple decades—used his father's senate connections to earn a draft deferment, not once but three times. Young passed bills that empowered the middle class, while Peterson amassed a fortune through his tech company. Nevertheless, Peterson utilized slick messaging and a prolific speaking schedule to hammer home his simple slogan: A New Era is Dawning.

Critics and foes alike mocked Peterson for his catchphrase, but it didn't seem to matter to the masses. In a country where the word *restless* could describe the constant state of most voters, Peterson seized on this and further agitated citizens who considered themselves most likely to go to the polls. Peterson ditched conventional thinking in attempting to appeal to undecided voters as the election drew nigh, instead opting for a closing campaign that spoke to the concerns of the people who would be casting ballots. And Peterson was winning big.

Young agreed on the spot when his party's leadership asked that he run. Despite Young not being the strongest possible candidate, every political expert acknowledged he would be the only person strong enough to halt Peterson's momentum before the election. But it wouldn't be an easy task in such a short amount of time.

The term "constitutional crisis" was used *ad nauseam* as news analysts discussed how Congress would handle the impending election. *Would the election be rescheduled? If so, for how long? Or were there no provisions for a case such as a major party's nominee sudden death in the short weeks before the first Tuesday in November?* The questions bandied about were answered quickly amidst a bitter partisan debate in Congress. The compromise came in the form of a law allowing for a one-month delay in order to maintain the dates for the electoral college voting and the subsequent inauguration in January.

But flipping through the preliminary polling reports, Young couldn't deny he needed help. Peterson's massive head start meant Young needed a November surprise to prevent his opponent from surging ahead any further. And even that didn't guarantee Young a fighting chance. Young despised wading into the dirty mire of politics, but he felt it couldn't be helped. Peterson presented a dangerous change in direction for the country, one Young surmised would make the country more vulnerable in many areas—foreign in-

fluence and terrorism both perched at the top of that
list. Young felt desperate. He hesitated to dial the
number and make the call.

It's for the good of the country.

The phone rang twice, and Young contemplated
hanging up and claiming that he dialed by mistake. But
as much as he hated what he was doing, his sense of
duty held fast.

"I can't believe you don't have more important
things to do," J.D. Blunt said as he answered. "Aren't
there rallies for you to attend?"

"Michaels is barely in the ground," Young said.
"My advisors at least wanted to wait a week before I
hit the campaign trail in earnest. Something about the
optics of it all."

"I guess they don't realize the future of the re-
public is at stake," Blunt said.

"You sound like a partisan hack."

Blunt chuckled. "If the shoe fits . . . No, seriously, I just think Peterson could make us vulnerable
to these terrorist pukes popping off bombs like they're
fireworks on the Fourth of July. I guaran-damn-tee
you that he'll eliminate Firestorm."

"That's why I called."

"You're not going to eliminate it, are you?"

"Of course not. But I need your help to make
sure none of what we talked about happens.

Firestorm needs to survive. And the only way that's going to happen is if I become President."

"Well, how can I be of service to you?"

Young sighed. "If things continue to hum along as they have, Peterson is going to win without attending another rally if he doesn't want to. So I need some help, if you know what I mean."

"I catch your drift. Big Peterson scandal in November would go a long way to squelching his momentum and casting you as the candidate the people should see you as—the champion for the every day American and a staunch warrior against terror. What more could any red-blooded citizen of this country ask for?"

"I'm hoping that's enough because I don't have the luxury of crafting some savvy slogan to woo voters. My message will be simple and straightforward: Peace and Prosperity for Generations to Come."

"The country will rally behind that kind of campaign."

"That's what I'm hoping for, but I'm also not naïve enough to think that Peterson is planning a takedown of me. He's going to cast me as another extension of Michaels and trot out all the tired attacks."

"At least Peterson doesn't have time to dig too deep on you."

"You know he won't find anything."

"I'll make sure he won't find this either. I've got some trusted contacts over at the NSA who feel likewise regarding Peterson. I'll give them a call and find out what they can unearth on him."

"Make it happen," Young said. "And don't contact me with any news about what you find. I want to at least have some plausible deniability."

"I'll keep you insulated from the whole ordeal. In fact, we were just speaking today about the election in general, and I was giving you advice as your friend, right?"

"Absolutely. Good luck, J.D."

Young hung up the phone and shuddered about what he just put into motion. He buzzed his secretary to bring him a cup of coffee then wondered if he'd ever be able to put what he'd just done behind him.

CHAPTER 4

Guantanamo Bay, Cuba

THE JEEP SKIDDED TO A HALT just outside the infamous Camp Delta. Home to some of the most vile terrorists in the world, the detention facility appeared intimidating. Given the backdrop of the exquisite blue water rolling ashore from the Caribbean Sea, the prison sat in stark contrast to its surroundings.

Alex pressed her hand on top of her hat, which the wind threatened to rip away. Hawk offered to take one of the bags she'd lugged to the facility for their interview with Tabari Sharaf.

"For all the flack this place catches, it sure is beautiful," Alex said as she scanned the area.

"I'd vacation here," Hawk said. "Of course, this beach would be more scenic if this eye sore wasn't here."

The base commander, Evan Patrick, cleared his throat as he gestured for his guests to continue.

"If this eye sore wasn't here, you'd have several more of these thugs to track down all across the desert. Besides, the Caribbean is full of better places to vacation."

Hawk nodded. "Can't argue with that."

"But we're not here to discuss that, now are we? You two have some business to conduct—or so I hear," Patrick said.

"Never been on a more important mission," Hawk said.

"Well, hopefully one of these numb nuts here can be of assistance to you," Patrick said, gesturing toward a nearby checkpoint. "After you."

Hawk and Alex walked side by side across the dusty safe zone. Hawk watched the prisoners on the other side of the series of barbed wire fences shuffle around. He decided that calling Camp Delta a *prison* was a misnomer, at least in the sense of any detention facility he'd ever seen in the U.S. The entire encampment seemed designed to create discomfort on every level. Sentries loomed over the compound, guns trained on the captives, ready to squeeze off several rounds should any mischief occur. The scant recreation area was completely fenced in, including the sky above. But that might have been five-star accommodations compared to their destination inside—Camp Five Echo, the facility's disciplinary block.

Accompanied by three guards, Patrick ushered Hawk and Alex through several posts inside until they reached the holding zone for non-compliant detainees.

"I've heard about this block," Alex whispered. "Human rights groups are always trying to shut it down."

"They're always trying to shut down everything," Hawk said. "They wouldn't be happy if these punks were put up in luxury hotels overlooking the ocean and being fed meals by world class chefs."

"Well, at least there's somewhat of an ocean view here."

They continued down a dim corridor until they reached cell B102. Patrick tugged on a small door, revealing an opening just large enough for him to see inside the room.

"You have some visitors, Tabari," Patrick said.

They waited about a minute for Tabari Sharaf to come to the door. The guards checked his shackles and then restrained his hands behind his back with a pair of handcuffs.

Sharaf remained solemn, refusing to look any of his captors in the eye as he trudged down the hall to a small conference room. He stopped on the other side of the table and slumped into his chair. Hawk and Alex settled into their seats across from Sharaf.

Patrick introduced them as lawyers with a human

rights group. Sharaf, who'd been imprisoned for more than five years, seemed to believe Patrick yet remained guarded until everyone but Hawk and Alex vacated the room.

Hawk conducted the conversation in Arabic, while Alex captured every word of it on her computer.

"For the record, it would be helpful if you repeated back our questions for documentation," Hawk began. "We want this conversation to be in your words."

Sharaf nodded.

"Let's begin with this one. Did you give up or were you captured against your will?"

"Did I give up or was I captured against my will? I was seized by those monsters out there. I was doing nothing but farming my land when they drove up on their armed vehicles and took me hostage. They dragged me away from my family. I've never even been a part of Al Hasib—and I never will. Al Hasib soldiers once stormed my house and took advantage of my wife and daughter right in front of me. You think I would ever have anything to do with them? Please believe me when I say this."

Hawk smiled slightly. "I'm here to gather as much information as possible. You feel free to tell me everything that might help your case." He glanced down at his notes. "Do you know the location of Karif Fazil's hideout?"

"Do I know the location of Karif Fazil's hideout? Now, I have a question for you. Who is Karif Fazil?"

"He is the leader of Al Hasib."

"Then how would I know who he is?"

Hawk scribbled down a note and glanced at Alex. "This is standard protocol. We need to be able to have all these questions answered in order to make your case. Now, the next one. What would you do if you were free?"

"What would I do if you were to set me free? I would return home to my family and try to rebuild our lives. Who knows what has happened to my wife and children since I've been gone. They could all be dead for all I know. Or they could be slaves of Al Hasib soldiers."

"Where did you live when you were captured?"

"Where did I live when I was captured? I lived in Iraq, near Basrah."

Hawk looked at Alex. She nodded at him. He returned his gaze to Sharaf.

"I think we have everything we need," Hawk said.

Sharaf scowled. "That's all? But I have so much more to tell you."

"This was all we needed to make our determination if we were going to take your case." Hawk turned toward the door. "Guards."

The door unlocked, and the trio of guards entered the room.

Sharaf stood but didn't move. "I can tell you more, so much more."

"This is enough," Hawk said again.

"When will you tell me if you will take my case?" Sharaf asked, his eyes pleading.

"We will pass the word back through the commanding officer of this facility," Hawk said. "Thank you for your time."

"But—but I'm not through," Sharaf said.

Alex waited until Sharaf left the room before she began splicing the conversation.

"Will you be able to make this work?" Hawk asked.

"I'll do my part, but this really isn't up to me," she answered, refusing to look up. "Labiib Nasri is the one who is going to determine if this is a successful operation or not."

Sharaf was just the means to an end. The real target was Nasri, who Hawk was counting on to pass a message on to Karif Fazil in order to flush him out into the open.

Patrick returned to the room and requested an update. "Did you get everything you needed?"

Hawk nodded. "We think so. But this all hinges on what happens tomorrow. Are you sure Nasri's lawyer is coming?"

"He hasn't missed a scheduled appointment yet," Patrick said. "And we don't make it easy on them if they cancel so close to the date."

"And you're certain he's passing messages to Fazil using his lawyer?"

"I'm never certain of anything regarding these psychopaths we have locked up here, but I'm confident the message will reach Fazil. What he does with that information is where things get tricky. From what I've learned in briefings about Fazil, he can be pretty unpredictable."

Hawk shrugged. "About some things, but he's very predictable in others, such as how close he'll get to the action."

"That chicken shit has no problems sending out others with suicide vests strapped to them, but he wouldn't dare slip arms through one if it was the only way he could accomplish his vision."

"The bastard wants to be alive to see it," Hawk said. "But he doesn't understand that I'll do anything to make sure he never sees even a sliver of his dream realized. And that means if I have to die, so be it."

"We think these terrorists fight like they have nothing to lose, but the reality is they are never willing to go the distance. They fight like they have far much more to lose than the free world. But despite what it may look like at times, the free world is full of too many good people who aren't going to lie down against some repressive regime. If history is a good indicator, Fazil and his ilk will fail soon as well."

"Sooner rather than later if I have any say in the matter."

"Let's just hope that Nasri does as we think he will—and Fazil, too."

Hawk nodded. "It's not a foregone conclusion, but we need to turn the tables on Fazil and get a leg up on him before it's too late."

Alex pounded the keyboard and stood. "We're all done here."

"Time for phase two," Hawk said.

"Right this way," Patrick said, gesturing toward the door.

The trio walked back down the long corridor and entered another building. Patrick gave a signal with his eyes when they were near Nasri's cell but eased back down the hallway.

"I can't believe it," Hawk said. "Sharaf just rolled over so easily."

"I know," Alex said. "What happened to jihad over family? He definitely doesn't have his priorities right."

"Play it one more time," Hawk said. "I want to hear his voice utter the words again."

"I know the location of Karif Fazil's hideout,"

Sharaf's voice said on the recording. "If you were to set me free, will you let me return home to my family and try to rebuild our lives?"

"Yes," Hawk's voice said. "I'll give you whatever you ask for within reason."

A few seconds of silence followed by Sharaf meekly saying, "Here it is."

"Thank you for these coordinates," Hawk replied.

Hawk was amazed at how Alex had managed to create the ambient background noise so that it sounded like he'd actually had this conversation with Sharaf. The truth was he'd recorded his responses prior to the meeting.

"Play it again," Hawk said loudly, gesturing for Alex to turn up the volume.

Near the end of the second time listening to the recording, Patrick ran up to them.

"What are you two doing?" he said. "You should wait before you start playing that recording here."

"What difference does it make? These guys here can't tell anyone," Hawk said with a dismissive wave.

"Don't be so sure of that. Prisoners here have some creative ways of getting messages out of here if they really want to."

"Fine," Hawk said, turning off the recording. He trudged along the corridor and entered the commons area, Alex and Patrick in tow.

"Think he took the bait?" Hawk asked.

A guard hustled over to Patrick and whispered something in his ear. Patrick smiled as the message was being conveyed. Once the guard left, Patrick repeated what he'd just heard to Hawk and Alex.

"Security footage showed Nasri staying in the shadows but turning his ear toward the small opening in the door. He was right there, listening to everything."

"Now, all he has to do is pass the message along," Alex said. "If Fazil is where we think he is, he won't be able to move without us knowing it."

CHAPTER 5

KARIF FAZIL STROKED JAFAR'S FEATHERS
and paced around his spacious bunker. Long before
Fazil began his assault on the western world, he had a
half dozen hideouts built throughout the Middle East.
Each one was built into the side of a mountain or in
an existing cave. The agrarian life nearby provided a
great cover for the construction of such structures,
transporting everything in and out on hoofed animals.
Fazil's stealthy building campaign and long-term planning insured that he remained off the Americans'
radar, both figuratively and literally. But when Fazil
burst onto the scene, he was more than prepared to
settle into the trenches for a prolonged fight.

"There, there," Fazil said, holding his hand out
with some seed in it for Jafar. "No need to make such
a raucous. You're safe in here with me."

This particular bunker was Fazil's favorite since it was built with Jafar in mind. His pet bird had plenty of room to soar around inside when the enemy was rumored to be sniffing around. But with this fortress's location in the mountainous desert terrain, Fazil hadn't even heard the slightest chatter about the Americans identifying his preferred site. He'd grown so confident that satellite imagery hadn't even picked up a trace of its presence that he sometimes let Jafar out to fly around before returning to the cave.

"Everyone is here, sir," one of Fazil's assistants said, interrupting Fazil and his intimate conversation with Jafar.

"Have them come in and sit down," Fazil said, refusing to turn around as he stared across the rocky landscape stretching out in front of him.

"Yes, sir," the assistant said before he exited the room.

Fazil waited until the doors closed before resuming his conversation with Jafar.

"Are you ready for this?" Fazil asked, stroking Jafar's head. "You're going to have an important role, and I'm really counting on you. Do you think you're up for it?"

Jafar cawed and swooped around the room in triumphant fashion.

Fazil broke into a hearty laugh. "I'll take that as a *yes*."

Jafar then lighted on Fazil's shoulder and mimicked Fazil's gaze into the distance.

A handful of Al Hasib's leaders filed into the room to get their orders from Fazil for their mission, an assignment Fazil called their most important to date. Fazil hesitated to attach such importance to what they were about to do because he considered everything Al Hasib did as vital to their overall operation. Each time he struck a blow against the Americans, he wanted to inflict maximum damage. Sometimes the fear he generated among the public was satisfaction enough that he'd succeeded in accomplishing his goals. But those had all shifted. No longer was Fazil going to be satisfied with leading his band of jihadist on simple ventures of terror. Fazil had become intent on bringing America to its knees in a way the country hadn't collectively experienced since that fateful day on September 11, 2001.

Fazil turned around and smiled as he noted everyone was already seated.

"Thank you for taking time off from your posts to come here and discuss the intricate details of a plan that is going to elevate the name *Al Hasib* on the lips of westerners," Fazil began. "No longer will we be considered a group begging for the attention some of those jihadists before us have attained. No, after we complete this operation, we will be both feared and revered. Never again will any country underestimate the ability of Al Hasib. And that in and of itself would be enough to declare a major victory. But I can assure you if we execute everything flawlessly, such accompanying accolades and attention will be secondary compared to the fear our name alone will invoke when spoken aloud."

Fazil held his hand up and coaxed Jafar to step onto it. The bird hopped onto Fazil's hand before taking flight and careening around the room.

"We have been suppressed for far too long, held back by our limitations, whether they were operational, personnel, or financial," Fazil said. "But all of those barriers have been removed. We have one of the most well-trained group of fighters in the world today. We have an ample supply of men to accomplish what we set out to do, thanks in large part to our recruiting efforts. And last but not least, our war chest is brimming with money. We want for nothing—and it is time to gather our forces and strike like we've never struck before.

"However, this won't be an operation that utilizes the power we possess. Instead, it will be an operation that takes full advantage of the power we've been able to harness. With one simple weapon, we can bring the world to its knees. Leaders from every nation will bow to us by the time we are finished, that much I can promise you."

The door across the room creaked open, and a man slipped inside. With his back to the wall, he eased his way around the room amidst the awkward silence. Fazil motioned for the man to come.

The man swallowed hard and took a deep breath before stalking across the floor as every gaze in the place was fixated on him.

"What's the meaning of this?" Fazil demanded in a soft whisper. "I thought I told you to never interrupt me."

"I wouldn't have come in here if it wasn't important."

Fazil sighed. "Very well then. Tell me what bit of information you think warrants such an interlude."

"We just received a message from Nasir's lawyer," the man began. "He just visited Nasir at Guantanamo Bay."

"And?"

"The lawyer said Nasir heard Tabari Sharaf divulge our location to the Americans."

"Is he sure of this?"

"Nasir's lawyer wanted me to convey to you that this is serious. He heard Sharaf tell the Americans with his own ears, according to the message I received. And that's not all."

Fazil gestured for his assistant to continue. "Go on."

"There's an armed drone that has been circling overhead for the past five minutes. Based on his flight pattern, I think it's safe to assume he knows we're here."

"Thank you," Fazil said. "You're dismissed."

"My friends, we seem to have the enemy crouching at our doorstep," Fazil said. "It was just reported that there's an armed U.S. drone soaring over us right now."

"We need to leave," one of the men said.

"Yes. Right now," said another as he stood.

"Sit back down," Fazil said as he threw his hand in the air. "We're not going anywhere."

CHAPTER 6

Washington, D.C.

BLUNT CHEWED ON HIS CIGAR and stared out the window of his new office suite. When Noah Young took over as acting president, he made sure to take care of Blunt so he could continue his work with Firestorm. And Blunt certainly couldn't argue with the view. The leaves were changing, and the city looked even more picturesque than it did when the cherry blossoms sprang.

But that wasn't even the best thing about the office to Blunt. Regaining the ability to use secured government phone lines made everything worth it. Nobody would be snooping on his conversations, at least not anyone affiliated with Congress or the military—or any other clandestine organization under the authority of the president. Such luxuries might come to an abrupt end, but Blunt determined to enjoy it while it lasted as well as take full advantage of it.

Digging up dirt on James Peterson proved more difficult than Blunt initially thought. Given enough time, Blunt could use his considerable resources to generate a full-blown controversy, complete with witnesses and signed affidavits. But time was in short supply for Young's sudden campaign. Blunt needed more than just dirt—he needed mud, the kind the media could roll around in and play with for more than just one twenty-four-hour cycle on the cable news networks.

Blunt had put out a few feelers to some of his trusted private investigators, if anything to see if there had been any buzz about what skeletons were hanging in Peterson's closet. With a well-documented success story, Peterson's rise to become a giant tech magnate was nothing new for the American public. But what he did on his rise to the top—or what he did once he got there—was of keen interest to Blunt. Of all the P.I.'s Blunt liked to hire, he knew he could always count on Charles Miller to deliver the goods.

"I got nothing for ya," Charles Miller told Blunt.

"Nothing? As in *nothing, nothing*?" Blunt asked, almost pleading.

"Zilch. The guy is as clean as a whistle."

"Now, you know if a guy is clean, he's been scrubbing his past."

"Don't I know that all too well," Miller said. "But I can just about guarantee you that you're going to have to fabricate something if you're going to catch James Peterson in some kind of scam."

"Fabricate something? Come on, Charles. You know I'd never do anything like that."

Miller chuckled. "Okay, J.D. Whatever you say. I'm just telling you this guy has covered all his bases. He must've had a cleaning crew working around the clock. I can't even find a chat room where anyone says something bad about him. No disgruntled employees. No jilted business partners. No messy divorces. Hell, even his adult children seem to like him."

"That has to be an act."

"Maybe they want to make sure Daddy doesn't leave them out of the will."

"Regardless, there has to be somebody somewhere willing to talk about the monster that is James Peterson, right?"

"I found one lady who seemed mildly interested in sharing her story about working for Peterson, one that she alleged was still filled with unwanted advances and other unseemly activity."

"So, what happened to her?"

"I've got an idea, but not an official story," Miller said. "On the night we were supposed to meet to document her story, she didn't show up. So, I got her address and drove to her house where a shiny new Mercedes-Benz was parked in the driveway. I knocked on the door, and she told me that I must be mistaken because she never agreed to tell me any story, let alone say anything negative about her wonderful boss, Mr. Peterson."

"You really are fighting an uphill battle, aren't you?"

"It's what I do all day long."

"Well, thanks for looking into it for me. If you do happen to hear of something else, please don't hesitate to call me."

"You got it," Miller said before he hung up.

Blunt was left with the silence and the heavy weight that accompanied it to ponder another possible direction. He stared at his phone for a few seconds, lingering on it and playing the conversation over in his head, a conversation he'd yet to have but one he desperately needed to have. He took one last deep breath before picking up the receiver again and placing another call.

"Trevor McDonald," the man said as he answered.

"Trevor, it's so good to hear your voice," Blunt said after removing the cigar from his mouth.

"Senator Blunt, is that you?" McDonald asked.

"Sure as I am sittin' here."

"Aww, man. To what pleasure do I owe your call, Senator?"

"What do you think about the Longhorns' chances of winning the conference this year? That game against Oklahoma was a classic."

"Hook 'em, Horns," McDonald said. "Best damn football team in the land. Who cares what the pollsters think, right?"

"Exactly. If they finish up strong, they'll be hoisting a championship trophy by season's end."

"Now, Senator, you know I'll gladly talk college football with you any time, but I have a feeling you called for a different reason, now didn't you?"

Blunt laughed. "Nobody could ever get anything by you, Trevor. That's why you're working for the NSA these days."

"I'd like to think it's because of all my hard work and dedication that I'm here today."

"Ah, you know what I mean. You've always been so damn tough to sneak anything by. Your father and I could never talk in code around you because you'd figure out what we were discussing in a matter of seconds."

"So, if you didn't call to talk about football—"

"All right, I'm getting to my point," Blunt said. "As much as I'd love to have an hour-long conversation over beer about our beloved football team, I do have some other pressing matters."

"I'm all ears."

"That's a good one, son," Blunt said. "You really are."

"I wasn't trying to make a joke. It's just an expression."

"And a fitting one for anybody that works at the NSA."

McDonald sighed. "Perhaps we should have this conversation over beers later tonight."

"No, no. I'll be brief."

"Go ahead then."

"I'm doing a little background check on our good friend James Peterson and was wondering if you happened to hear anything untoward regarding the presidential candidate."

"Senator, you're not asking me what I think you're asking?"

"I'm just inquiring to see if there are any chinks in his armor, so to speak. Just wondering if any rumors or stories have flitted across your desk as of late."

"Look, not to be rude, Senator, but I don't feel comfortable with this conversation. This isn't really appropriate—not to mention legal—for me to be discussing with you. Maybe you were used to these kinds of calls when you were on the defense committee, but I think we both know that the information you're requesting isn't the kind you can have access to."

Blunt grunted. "If you only knew. Well, I get it. You're trying to do the right thing, and I guess I can't fault you for that. But if you happen to come across something that you think would be useful and want to call me on your own free time, let me give you my number."

Blunt recited his cell before wishing McDonald a good afternoon. After hanging up, Blunt stood back up and shoved the cigar into his mouth. He chewed on the Cuban tobacco for a few minutes in silence, contemplating his next move.

No one is that squeaky clean.

CHAPTER 7

Washington, D.C.

ALEX LOOPED THE DRONE around the position of Karif Fazil's suspected hideout in Iraq and let out a few choice words when nothing of interest appeared on the screen. Caves, caves, and more caves. She wanted to lower the drone's altitude, but if she was right about where Fazil was laying low, she would fly right into an easy shot for one of Al Hasib's guards. One blast from a rocket propelled grenade launcher and her eyes and ears from the sky would go up in a plume of black smoke.

"Are you sure you're not seeing *anything* out there?" Alex asked Hawk.

Hawk, who'd been dispatched to the region, was a quarter of a mile away from the front of Fazil's suspected underground location. She calculated the distance as the drone circled around on its previous approach.

"I can see the entrance," Hawk said. "There's no reason you couldn't just light it up right now."

Alex sighed. "This is the last Al Hasib hideout that we have confirmed on the ground. If I obliterate it and he's not there, we'll never know where he'll go into hiding next."

"But if he's in there . . ."

"Hawk, I thought you wanted to watch him die."

"It's the only way to be a hundred percent sure that he's dead. Otherwise, we're left with picking over the bones of a bunch of Al Hasib guards and hoping a DNA test matches. I'd never be sure."

"Exactly. So, why have me blast this place now?"

"I'm close enough that I could verify Fazil's identity now while his body was still warm."

Alex huffed a laugh through her nose. "If I blast this place now, you'll be lucky to identify him with dental records."

"At least it would put an end to my visits to this godforsaken part of the world."

"I'm not doing it," she said. "Not until you can get a visual on him. It's too risky."

"Fine," he said. "I'll get closer."

"You better make it quick. I can't keep this drone in the air all day. There are limitations to what I can do."

"Just fly it elsewhere for a while. Give me some time to work. I'll notify you as soon as I see something, and then you can come in and finish the job. Deal?"

"These things aren't solar powered," she said. "I can't just fly it forever. At some point, I'm going to have to guide this bird back to the base."

"You're gonna have to trust me on this," Hawk said. "Watch me on the satellite feed. You'll see just how close I am before I let you know I have visual confirmation."

"And how exactly are you going to entice Fazil to come out?"

"I've got a few ideas—none of which will work if you keep buzzing this drone around his hideout. Are you with me?"

"Yeah, yeah. I'll take her elsewhere. But you better work quick. Based on my calculations, I've got maybe a half hour left before I'll have to send her back to the base and park her."

"Roger that."

Alex typed in a few more new coordinates, sending off the drone in a different direction. All she could do now was wait—and hope.

CHAPTER 8

Washington, D.C.

BLUNT SAT AT THE BAR and glanced at the football game airing on the television affixed to the wall. The Packers were hosting the Redskins on a snowy Lambeau Field. The bartender made eye contact with Blunt before glancing down at his glass.

"Time for another?" the bartender asked.

Blunt swirled the dregs of his bourbon around and shrugged.

"Why not? Looks like I got stood up anyway."

"Blind date?"

"That might be the only way I get a date these days," Blunt deadpanned. "She'd have to be blind. I'm not exactly the prettiest thing on the shelf."

"Love isn't always about looks," the bartender said as he placed another glass in front of Blunt.

"But it sure does help."

"Help what?" asked a man behind Blunt.

Blunt turned around to see Trevor McDonald a few feet away wearing a big grin.

"What?" McDonald asked. "You didn't think I was going to stand you up, did you?"

"I was beginning to wonder."

McDonald settled onto the stool next to Blunt and ordered a drink.

"Sorry about earlier," McDonald said. "If there's one place you shouldn't be making plans to skirt the law, it's inside NSA headquarters."

"I know. I'm sorry. I put you in a difficult situation, and that's my fault. You did the right thing."

"I still don't feel right about this whole thing, but given the circumstances, I felt like someone needed to know, someone who would actually do something about it."

Blunt took a pull on his drink. "So, no one at the NSA would take any action on what you found?"

McDonald looked over his left shoulder and then his right before proceeding. "Let's just say that not everyone there shares the same political views we do."

Blunt waved dismissively. "It's not about political affiliation. It's about doing what's right. I don't care what party a candidate is in. If he—or she—needs to be shut down, then someone needs to do it. And it might as well be me."

"Before I tell you this, you have to answer me one question."

"Fire away."

"You're not just doing this because you're close with Noah Young, are you?"

"My relationship with Noah Young is incidental in this case," Blunt said. "I've heard some pretty rotten things from insiders on James Peterson. He puts on a good face, but behind the scenes, he's a ball buster. It's his way or the highway."

"That seems to be a common trait among self-made billionaires."

"It's also the recipe for disaster when it comes to dealing with a divided electorate and a world rife with terrorists who know how to push all the right buttons. I'd give him six months before he has the world at each other's throats and ready to start the next big world war."

"So you think you can stop him?"

"Depends upon what kind of information you give me tonight."

"Well, you're going to love what I'm about to tell you."

Blunt arched his eyebrows and gestured for McDonald to continue.

"Okay, no one else at the NSA seems to be very concerned with the incidental information I've collected on Peterson, but I think it's quite serious."

"How so?"

"He's meeting with a Russian ambassador in a few days."

Blunt took another pull on his drink. "And why were you listening in on this particular ambassador?"

"He's proposing a deal to Peterson in exchange for help with the election."

"Financial help?"

McDonald nodded. "That's the rumor. We haven't been able to confirm it."

"So, you exposed him?"

"It might seem politically motivated at this point, but there are some people I know who seem genuinely concerned with the possibility that Peterson could find his way to the Oval Office."

"Count me among those who are concerned."

"I thought you might be, but I'm very serious. There are some other things happening that I'm not at liberty to discuss."

"What kind of things?"

"The kind of things that could land a man in federal prison for a very long time."

"Peterson?"

McDonald stared at his drink and didn't say a word.

"Someone close to Peterson?"

McDonald remained quiet, staring up at the television.

"Okay, fine. You don't want to talk about it in public. I understand. But you need to give me something to go on rather than a vague and cryptic comment. If I'm going to hunt, I need to know what I'm hunting for."

"Just expose Peterson for the fraud that he is," McDonald said. "That will save everyone a lot of trouble."

Blunt smiled. "I can do that. All I need from you is the pertinent information to make it all happen."

* * *

NOAH YOUNG HAD YET to move into the White House, deciding to remain at Number One Observatory Circle. The official residence of the vice president located on the grounds of the U.S. Naval Observatory was quaint and less monitored. While a stunning home on the inside with all the bells and whistles one would expect, the house appeared rather modest on the outside. Young contemplated moving into the White House permanently, but he decided against it when his party gave him the green light to take Michaels's place on the ticket. The last thing Young wanted was to come across as an entitled politician. Being well within his right to live there, but refusing to do so out of respect for Michaels's family and for the office itself played well with the American public. But Young had his own reasons for refusing his rightful residence.

The vice president's home had far more latitude in what Young could get away with. Making secret phone calls and directing intelligence gathering ops at 1600 Pennsylvania Avenue required stealthier moves than Young was accustomed to making—and he knew that. He preferred to handle the dark matters of running a campaign away from the limelight.

He slipped into his study and dialed the number of a former Air Force friend who was working in private security in the nation's capital.

"This is Geller."

"As in Frank Geller?"

"Noah Young? Is that really you?"

Young chuckled. "It's been a while, hasn't it?"

"Only a couple decades or so," Geller said. "I would ask you how you got my number, but I doubt there's much that the acting president of the United States can't get if he wants it."

"Some of the stories you hear are highly exaggerated, trust me."

"Well, how the heck are ya? I just can't believe you're the president now."

"*Acting* president," Young corrected. "I still have some work to do if I'm going to become a permanent fixture in the Oval Office."

"Yeah, I saw the latest polls. Things aren't really going your way, are they?"

"According to my campaign manager, I'm being punished for all of Michaels's sins, complicit or not. But all is not lost just yet."

"So, how do you plan on turning that around?"

"Funny that you should ask," Young said. "That's actually the reason for my call."

"If you're looking for my vote, I promise you'll get it."

Young laughed softly. "Actually, I'm looking for something even more helpful than that."

"What do you need?"

"I need you to do something for me that will stop James Peterson from becoming president."

"I gathered as much, but I hope you're not suggesting that I do something to harm him physically," Geller said. "I know I got into a few tussles when we were serving together, but those days are long behind me."

"Not anything *physically*, but definitely something that will harm his political campaign. Or to be more blunt—shine a light on what he's really up to."

"You want me to sabotage the election?"

"No, no. Just listen before you start making a thousand wild guesses."

"Okay. I'm all ears."

"Good," Young said. "Peterson is aligning with some of our foreign political foes. And doing so makes him susceptible as President. We just need to nip it all in the bud so we don't have to spend the next four years wondering if Peterson's allegiances lie elsewhere. I have it on good authority that he's secretly meeting with a Russian ambassador tonight. I'm not privy to the nature of their conversation, but I know it doesn't look good. He's hiding this meeting from the reporters covering his campaign and making sure it's completely off the books."

"Maybe he's trying to shore up relations so after the election that doesn't come as such a shock," Geller said.

"And maybe my Aunt Gladys will sprout wings and fly off her rocker so she doesn't have to use her walker to get around any more. I love how you see the best in people, Geller. But that isn't the case here. Peterson is doing some dangerous things right now, and if we don't expose him, our country could elect an even bigger traitor than Conrad Michaels."

"That's a bold statement."

"And a true one. You have to trust me on this one, Geller. I might be a politician now, but you know I've never lied to you. And I'm not lying about this."

Geller was silent for a moment. "I believe you. Just tell me what you want me to do."

"I want you to set up a hidden camera in the room where Peterson is going to be meeting with a Russian ambassador."

"That's it?"

"Just make sure you don't get caught entering the building or on any of their security cameras. It's going to be a big deal."

"I can handle that," Geller said. "Just text me the address. My phone is as secure as it can be."

"Thanks," Young said. "I'll get right on it. Time is of the essence."

Young hung up and leaned back in his chair. He stared at the oak tree outside his window as a faint smile crept across his face.

CHAPTER 9

Iraq, undisclosed location

HAWK WAITED UNTIL THE DRONE vanished on the horizon before making his way closer to Fazil's compound. There was something about a solo op that he found both terrifying and exhilarating. Without any backup, Hawk had to rely on his wits and training to navigate deep into hostile enemy territory. Alex could only do so much flying a drone from several thousand miles away. If he got caught, Hawk would either be condemned to captivity or possibly death. The margin for error had been reduced to zero. He had no friends in this part of the world controlled by Al Hasib, at least none he knew of. He had no favors to call in. He didn't even have official permission from his own country to be in Iraq, though Pentagon brass would treat him like a hero if he succeeded.

But the *if* was big, hanging in the balance. The

odds of success were weighted in Al Hasib's favor.

Hawk slunk behind a rock and pulled out his binoculars to survey the area.

"The drone should be out of ear shot now," Alex said over the coms.

"Uh, huh," Hawk said. "The only thing I hear now are some trucks way off in the distance and a snake slithering at my six."

"Those things move quick from what I hear. You might want to keep going."

Hawk spun around on his heel and stomped on the snake's head. He ground it into the sand until the snake crunched beneath the weight of his boot.

"Problem solved," Hawk announced before returning his focus to the supposed location in the mountains.

"Did you really have to do that?" Alex asked.

"Yes. Yes, I did. You can't exactly med-evac me out of here if I were to get bitten by one of these creatures," Hawk said. "I'm doing what I need to do to survive."

"It was kind of a joke."

"Sorry, but I'm not in the mood right now. I'm now about two hundred meters from the opening of the hideout."

"And you can confirm that this is an Al Hasib location?"

"Sure as I'm sitting here," Hawk said. "They disguised the entrance very well and are using natural features from the mountain to shield the door from view. There's even a portion of the mountain that's carved out, big enough for them to store several large tactical vehicles in as well as a few transport trucks."

"You see anything else? Any people?" Alex asked.

"Not yet, but—wait a minute. The door is opening, and someone is walking out onto the patio area."

"Recognize him?."

"*Sonofabitch*. It's Fazil."

"You've gotta be kidding me."

"I already told you I wasn't in a joking mood."

"Do you have a shot?"

Through his binoculars, Hawk studied Fazil. With his bird Jafar perched on his shoulder, the Al Hasib leader strode forward. He held his head high as he surveyed the desert area sprawled out in front of him. Apparently satisfied with the environment, he looked at Jafar and nodded. Jafar flapped his wings and squawked before taking flight and soaring away from the opening. Jafar climbed higher and higher, circling the area for a couple minutes.

Hawk froze, taking the whole scene in. His gaze bounced between Fazil and Jafar in an effort to determine just how long the interaction would last. On the third trip around the area, something spooked Jafar. Instead of continuing his circuitous route, he broke it off and flew straight back to Fazil. Looking furtively at the landscape for a few seconds, Fazil raced back inside with Jafar nestled on his shoulder.

"What happened to the drone?" Hawk asked.

"She's still in a holding pattern several miles away," Alex answered. "Why?"

"Because Fazil's little pet bird looked like it was dive bombing him for a second, and then Fazil peered out in the direction I last saw the drone before darting back inside. It was strange, to say the least."

"I don't think anything is ever normal with that man."

"That's a fact, but I think the bird must've seen *something*."

"You think there's someone else out there with you?"

Hawk examined his surroundings once more through his binoculars. "If there is, I'm not seeing any signs of anyone."

Alex didn't respond. Hawk heard clicking sounds over his com, likely from Alex typing furiously on her keyboard.

"What is it?" Hawk asked.

"I'm seeing some heat signatures on the back side of the mountain," she said. "It's kind of weird, but it looks like there's an overhang about twenty feet off the ground."

"So you think there's another entrance?"

"It would appear so," she said. "But don't just go running in there. I need to analyze some more data here from this satellite image."

"Roger that." Hawk slipped his binoculars into his pack and stayed low as he crept across the desert floor.

"Hawk? Hawk? What are you doing now? You know I can see you, right?"

Hawk smiled and kept moving.

"Would you answer me?"

"Gotta keep a low profile now," he whispered. "If you can see me, you know I'm getting closer to the hideout."

"I'm not done studying these images, Hawk. This isn't funny."

"You were the one cracking jokes earlier today, not me. I'm serious as a heart attack."

"And so am I when I tell you that it's not a wise decision to go charging into the compound."

Hawk stopped behind a rock and eased into a prone position. "What choice do we have at this point? We know Karif Fazil is here. You could just obliterate the place. But I have to get the information. We need to know what he's going to do with that weapon. If he places it in the Strait of Hormuz, all hell is going to break loose, and we'll be on the precipice of another conflict in the Middle East."

"I get it, but I'm also concerned there are other ways to get this information."

"Such as . . . ?"

"I think it'd be easy to hack into the security mainframe and listen in on their meetings," she said.

"There's one problem with that," Hawk said. "I'm here and you're not. And believe me when I say this, but I'd love to have you here to do that. Unfortunately, that's not an option right now, and I need you to guide me to wherever you're seeing these heat signatures."

"Okay, fine. But it's only one heat signature—at least one human heat signature. There's a smaller one, too."

"Probably Fazil and his little pet."

"That'd be my guess, too, but I can't verify that."

"If he stays where he is, I'll be able confirm it's Fazil in less than five minutes."

"Roger that."

Hawk resumed his trek around the mountain, cutting through a narrow pass in the wall likely caused by erosion. Alex guided him through the area, assuring him that there weren't any guards in his path. After a few minutes, Hawk eased into position and pulled out his binoculars again to inspect the heat signatures Alex had identified.

"Are you still seeing those heat sigs?" Hawk asked.

"They're showing up on my screen. Why? Are you not seeing anyone?"

"Just give me a second."

Hawk studied the area, swinging from left to right. On his first pass, he didn't see anyone on the clever balcony tucked beneath a cavern and hidden from view. Hawk took a moment to marvel at the engineering feat required to create such a hidden feature that gave Fazil and his men access to the outdoors without being caught by any prying satellite cameras.

"Hawk, I'm seeing two new heat sigs near your position. Do you copy?"

"Loud and clear."

"You're not thinking about going in there right now, are you?"

"Alex, I'm not going to get many more chances like this, if at all. I've got to seize this one."

"That's not a good idea. We have no idea what's inside. I suggest you wait it out and see if you can capture one of the guards and get the information from him. That's what this mission was all about, not settling some score with Fazil."

"Sometimes you've gotta buck conventional wisdom and take the bull by the horns."

"Sometimes wisdom is living to fight another day."

"Wish me luck."

"Hawk!" Alex said.

He turned the volume on his com down low and snuck closer.

The balcony area was about three feet off the ground, a concrete slab poured over the jagged cave floor. The sky was still visible, albeit a shaded view by the cavernous overhang. But the edges remained rather dark, perfect for lying in wait.

Hawk waited until one of the guards had wandered aimlessly near the edge before springing into action. The man poked his head over the railing for a cursory look only to have someone reach up and jerk him over it. Hawk yanked the man onto the rocks below, bashing his head against a jagged feature. He didn't have a chance to scream before he was knocked out and likely dead.

Hawk eased eye level with the balcony floor and waited for the other guard to notice his friend was missing. Fazil wasn't paying any attention, instead engrossed on a phone call. Pacing around the balcony, Fazil waived his arms around as he spoke. While Hawk wasn't quite close enough to decipher the topic of conversation, he could tell from Fazil's body language that the Al Hasib leader wasn't pleased.

A moment later, the other guard noticed he was patrolling the area alone. As the dumbfounded expression swept across his face, he called out for his friend by name. As each second dripped past, the guard furrowed his brow. He raced to the edge and scanned the surrounding area.

Hawk watched intently as Fazil remained talking on the phone, his back turned as the entire situation unfolded. His relaxed nature led Hawk to believe that Fazil felt secure in his hideout, even after something spooked Jafar.

When the second guard neared the edge, his eyes widened as they met Hawk's.

Using both hands, Hawk grabbed the man by his shirt and pulled down hard. The guard toppled over the railing and let out a faint yelp before crashing to the ground with more velocity than the first guard.

Hawk checked both their pulses before setting his sights on the real prize. In a smooth motion, Hawk placed both his hands on the rail and pulled himself up, throwing his legs over onto the balcony and landing softly. Weapon drawn, Hawk eased up behind Fazil before inserting the gun barrel into the back of Fazil's head.

"Not another move or another sound," Hawk said.

"Brady Hawk," Fazil announced. "I should have known you would come racing into danger yet again. So, it wasn't enough that you escaped with your life the last time you came hunting for my underwater weapons system."

"It's not exactly yours."

"Police of the world, are we? Sounds just like your arrogant government. Sadly, your jurisdiction means nothing here, even if your country did help the Iraqis get rid of a tyrant."

"I don't have time for your lectures," Hawk said.

Fazil eased his hand into his pocket.

"I said not another move," Hawk said.

"Or what? You'll shoot me and not get the information you came here for? If you wanted me dead, you would've never introduced yourself, at least not so personally as you have here."

"I'm not here to make small talk. I'm here to find out where you've placed that mine weapon."

"You are relentless, I'll give you that. A hopeless romantic, I would surmise. You and little Alex holding hands and believing that you've made the world a safer place."

"I'm only going to give you one more chance," Hawk said. "Where is the weapon?"

Fazil raised his hands in surrender and turned around cautiously before coming face to face with Hawk.

"You mean *this* weapon?" Fazil said before tapping his watch. An electric charge bolted from his timepiece.

Hawk convulsed violently as he crumpled to the

ground, where he twitched and turned for nearly half a minute.

Fazil wore a big grin as he loomed over Hawk and watched him until he finally stopped.

"Looks like it's time for you to answer some questions for me," Fazil said before whistling for a pair of guards inside to give him a hand.

Hawk wanted to say something. He wanted to fight back. But he could scarcely move, much less put up enough of a fight to stand a chance. The last thing he saw before he blacked out was Fazil's fist.

CHAPTER 10

BLUNT CHECKED HIS WATCH and prepared for the peep show that would mark the downfall of James Peterson's bid to become the president. In less than five minutes, Peterson would stride into a room with a Russian ambassador, discuss things no candidate should be discussing with him, and torpedo an election bid. If Blunt liked popcorn, he would've popped a big bowl's worth and sat back to watch the entertaining end. But he preferred scotch and fixed himself a glass in preparation of the event.

Pacing around the room, Blunt considered calling Alex to find out about Hawk's operation behind enemy lines. But Blunt didn't want to miss a second of the conversation.

Two minutes.

He took a long pull on his glass and settled into

his chair behind his desk to watch. While he was staring at the screen, his door burst open and a half dozen FBI agents raced into the room.

"What's the meaning of this?" Blunt demanded as he stood.

A final agent entered the room and stared at Blunt. "Sorry about the intrusion, Senator, but I'm Special Agent Renfroe. and you're under arrest for breaking the National Security Act."

"What the hell are you talking about? I'm a patriot."

"You're a patriot who's under arrest, sir," Renfroe said coolly. "We can do this the easy way or the hard way. I'd rather not walk you out of this building in handcuffs, but it's up to you."

"You're making a big mistake," Blunt said with a growl. "Let me get my cane."

Blunt eased into his old man act and shuffled across the room. He picked up his cane and shook it at Renfroe.

"You're making a mistake, Agent Renfroe," Blunt said. "How can I even get arrested for this? The National Security Act forbids government agencies from spying on American citizens. You're probably unaware that I don't work for the government any more."

"So, you're not denying that you were spying on someone?" Renfroe asked.

"I want to speak to my lawyer," Blunt said as he hobbled toward the door.

"Oh, you'll get to speak to your lawyer," Renfroe said. "You're not going to be mistreated in any way."

"This is wrong, so wrong," Blunt grumbled.

Blunt followed Renfroe and his team onto an elevator and descended to the bottom floor. The spectacle of a well-known former senator escorted by federal agents drew long glances, some of which were accompanied by gaping mouths. A few other people pulled out their cell phones and captured video of the event. A somber Blunt kept his head down and trudged along toward a waiting vehicle.

"This is going to be the end of your career, Renfroe."

Renfroe used the mirror on the passenger side visor to make eye contact with Blunt, who was wedged between a pair of agents.

"Comfy back there, Senator?" Renfroe asked.

Blunt sneered and turned to look out the window. As the SUV was pulling away, Blunt saw several people running up alongside the vehicle as they held out their phones to continue documenting the moment.

"You should've just perp walked me right through the front door," Blunt said. "It wouldn't have been any less of a circus than the one you just created.

I hope you're enjoying this final ride as an FBI agent. Some powerful people are going to be pissed that you're intervening like this."

"I find it interesting that you've yet to deny any of the charges," Renfroe said.

"How can I deny something for which I can't be charged?" Blunt asked. "It's almost like double jeopardy. I'm not even eligible to break this law since I don't work for a government agency."

"If you want to direct your anger at anyone, maybe you should consider the people who fingered you," Renfroe said. "I know you're really upset that you got caught, but you're not really that angry at me."

"No one turned me in," Blunt said. "The people I work with are loyal to me to a fault—every last one of them."

"Are you sure about that, Senator? Sometimes, it doesn't take much for someone to roll over on you."

"I'm as sure about that as I'm sure that I'm sitting here talking with you about your ridiculous theories. Whoever authorized this is overstepping their bounds."

Blunt rode the rest of the way in silence. When they arrived at FBI headquarters, a small crowd of reporters had gathered on the front steps. Once the agents opened the door for Blunt, the media members swarmed on them, shoving cameras and microphones

HARD TARGET | 91

in Blunt's face. He turned aside and shielded himself with his coat.

"Senator Blunt, what do you have to say for yourself?" one reporter asked.

"Senator, do you plan to fight these charges?" another inquired.

Blunt lumbered ahead, plowing through the frothing press corps on his way up the steps. He glanced to his left and noticed a small lectern set up with the FBI director making his way to it.

"The director is ready to make his remarks," a woman announced, drawing the attention of all the reporters. They scurried over to the director and worked quickly to set up their cameras to capture the announcement.

"What's that all about?" Blunt asked one of the agents.

"Oh, that?" asked the agent. "The director is making a statement about your arrest."

Blunt let out a string of expletives before entering the building and being subjected to a search by security personnel. Once Blunt was permitted to pass through the metal detectors, he was whisked away to a holding room.

Still fuming, Blunt sat with his arms crossed. An agent entered the room and placed a cup of coffee in front of him.

"Here you go, Senator," he said as he nudged the drink toward Blunt. "I wasn't sure, but I guessed you aren't a cream and sugar kind of guy."

"I'm not a coffee kind of guy," Blunt said and then grunted to punctuate his displeasure.

"Well, I'll get this out of your way then," the man said before snatching the cup and exiting the room.

Blunt stared at the clock on the far wall. The faint ticking sound irked him, serving more as a torture device than an informational tool. He didn't care what time it was. All he cared about was talking with his lawyer and clearing up this mess that was sullying a respectable reputation.

Another half hour passed before a knock on the door was followed by a familiar face.

Blunt glared at the man as he entered the room and sat down at the table across from him. It was Justin Frazier, head of the NSA.

"If you had anything to do with this, I swear I'm gonna choke you to death with my bare hands," Blunt said.

Frazier gave a coy smile. "It's nice to see you too, J.D."

CHAPTER 11

Washington, D.C.

HAWK, CAN YOU HEAR ME?" Alex said into her coms as she stared at her monitor after he disappeared into the shadows beneath a craggy rock face. She waited for a few seconds, hoping to hear something in her earpiece. Instead, she broke the silence when she slammed her fist down on her desk and let a few choice words fly. She paced around the room and tried to come up with a reasonable explanation for why he would charge into Fazil's compound and go dark at the same time.

Why doesn't he ever listen to me?

Watching Hawk break protocol and venture into enemy territory wasn't a new experience. But that didn't make it any less painful to endure. The wondering and speculating for even just a few minutes always drove her crazy. She concluded that she might not be the same way if he were just another operative she was handling. But she and Hawk had history—and something else, though giving it a label seemed juvenile. In moments like these, she realized just how much she cared for him. Alex always handled her job like a professional, but everything seemed heightened when he was in danger and she was unable to help.

But there is something I can do this time.

She took a deep breath and settled back into her chair. Calling up the drone's virtual cockpit, she resumed control of the machine.

Come on, Hawk. Show me something.

She turned the plane back around and then glanced at the monitor connected to the satellite. The screen was blank.

"Not right now," she said with a growl.

Switching to a different keyboard, she typed furiously to get the image back. She attempted to re-task the satellite so she could maintain visual contact of Hawk's location with something other than the drone's grainy camera. But her attempts were rebuffed when a box appeared with the dreaded words no hacker ever wanted to see: Access Denied.

Alex cursed as she went back to the controls of the drone. A few seconds later, she was frozen out of the drone as well.

"Damn it," she said. "Somebody's onto me."

On the street below, she heard a honk and a man yelling. Alex leaned over her desk and saw a dark van with several FBI agents in tactical gear rushing toward her apartment building.

She sprang into action, shutting down her laptop and initiating memory wipe protocol for her desktop computer. She checked the deadbolts on the front door and rushed back to check on the status of the hard drive erasure. Once it hit eighty percent, she heard footsteps in the hallway. At ninety percent, she heard a knock on the door and a man announcing himself with the FBI and requesting entry. She grabbed a blanket and threw it over the machine, hoping the extra time it took to locate her computer might be enough to help the system finish removing any incriminating evidence.

With her laptop tucked securely in a bag slung across her shoulder, Alex raced toward her hiding spot before clambering up into a large vent shaft. She'd practiced her escape several times in the event of a raid—and she was thankful for the foresight she had to develop such a procedure.

She heard the first loud thump of the FBI's battering ram crashing against her door.

In a matter of seconds, she was safely inside. She contorted her body, turning around so she could face the room below.

Another thump on the front door.

After she secured the screws on the vent, she slid back into the shadows. She was close enough to see anyone in the room but deep enough in the shaft that no one would be able to see her with a cursory glance.

The next thump was accompanied by the sound of wood splintering.

They're in.

Alex scooted farther back down the vent and held her breath. She decided she didn't care to know how many agents there were. The imminent danger was sufficient enough to scare her away from seeing the room. The only thing that mattered was avoiding capture so she could get back to helping Hawk.

As she eased her way down the duct, she heard an electric screwdriver whirring loudly. She squinted as she tried to see what was happening—an agent was removing the vent cover. It clanked as it hit the floor.

The agent shoved a flashlight into the vent and peered into it.

"I think I found something," he said.

Alex swallowed hard but didn't dare move—or breathe.

CHAPTER 12

Iraq, undisclosed location

HAWK RESISTED OPENING HIS EYES as long as he could. The burlap bindings wrapped around his wrists and ankles gave him a picture of his situation before he even saw a thing. Seated in a wooden chair, Hawk's arms were pinned behind him. A damp musty smell overwhelmed his senses.

"You can't keep your eyes closed forever," Karif Fazil said before he kicked at Hawk's leg.

Hawk relented and his gaze met Fazil's. The room was lit with a single lightbulb that dangled from the ceiling directly behind Fazil. With Jafar perched on his shoulder, the Al Hasib leader stooped over and looked eye-level at his prisoner.

"I knew you were brash and daring, but I never figured to add stupid to the adjectives I'd use to describe the great Brady Hawk," Fazil said as he stood and paced in front of Hawk. "On second thought, perhaps we should rethink inclusion of the word *great* when describing you. Such a blunder—a serious underestimation of your enemy—is not exactly what a great operative does."

"I guess you haven't met any great ones, have you?"

Fazil smiled. "Why? Because they all end up dead at your hands?"

Hawk narrowed his eyes but remained silent.

"Well, your bravado is also noted, particularly given your situation. Arrogant to the bitter end, though the end won't come quite as quickly as you'd like."

"There's a drone outside that will obliterate this facility any minute now," Hawk said. "If there's a fool in this room, it's you."

"My, the bold statements don't stop, do they? You're willing to spout off anything to rile me up, aren't you? However, there's one problem with your statement—it's not true. That drone is long gone. And I suspect it was commandeered by your little girlfriend. The military likely has no idea what it was doing out here."

"I wouldn't be so sure."

"Well, I won't be here for long, so it won't matter much. But you, on the other hand, consider this your final resting place," Fazil said as he held up some seeds for Jafar to eat. The bird pecked at them until he was satisfied and resumed his stoic position.

"I don't intend to be here very long either," Hawk said. "You're going to have to kill me now or I'm going to kill you."

Fazil broke into a hearty laugh. "I love it when a man has no regard for reality. I like to call such people *Americans*. But don't let me stop you. This comedy act is quite entertaining."

"I don't make empty threats."

"Your words certainly ring hollow given the fact that you're all tied up, weaponless, defenseless, and lacking any sort of backup," Fazil said. "One can only assume that you are here on your own in an *unauthorized* capacity."

"In America, we have a popular saying for people who *assume*. Maybe you've heard it before."

"I know that one all too well. And look at you here. You're living proof that the saying is correct. You operated under the assumption that you'd be able to get to me out here, that my guard would be down even after you dispatched two of my men. So, here you are, *Brady Hawk*."

"Just shoot me and get this over with. The real torture is listening to you drone on and on as if you've actually accomplished something."

"I've caught you, haven't I? That's something," Fazil said before waving dismissively at Hawk. "But I have actual plans to torture you in more meaningful ways before I take your pathetic excuse for a life."

"Watching you fail isn't exactly torture."

"I won't fail this time, mark my word. And you're going to watch me triumph until your dying breath. And that'll be the last thing you'll see. Now, if you'll excuse me, I need to go save the world . . . from people like you."

Fazil pulled on the string behind him, quenching the light in the room. His footsteps echoed as he walked across the floor and exited, slamming the door behind him.

Hawk let out an exasperated breath, left to contemplate his fate in the dark. He couldn't allow Fazil's words to bother him, though the terrorist cell leader was right—Hawk had acted brashly and made some costly assumptions. The plan was never to assault Fazil personally, just get information from one of his men about the location of the weapons system before retreating back to safety.

But Hawk let his thirst for blood get in the way. Fazil and his men had become an ever-present danger to American interests both at home and abroad. Seeing an opportunity—albeit a dangerous one—Hawk seized it and was left to lament his decision in an Al Hasib holding cell.

Hawk realized his com was missing, certainly confiscated immediately after he went down at the hands of Fazil's crafty taser. Without a way to reach Alex, Hawk could only imagine what she was thinking. Any rescue attempts would have to be conducted on her own and strongly ill-advised. He knew she was smarter than that—as long as she didn't let her emotions cloud her judgment.

And as difficult as Hawk's situation seemed, he needed to focus on the two positive aspects of his capture. First, he was still alive. Second, Fazil suggested he was going to let Hawk live long enough to see presumably some vile act of terrorism against America. And as long as there was breath in him, he figured he had a chance to escape and turn the tables on Fazil. But such goals were far more easily imagined than accomplished.

His thoughts were interrupted when light flooded the room as the door swung open. Two men lumbered toward Hawk. One reached up and pulled on the string, illuminating the single bulb. It swung back and forth, casting dancing shadows on the walls around them.

Neither one of the men said a word as they circled Hawk. They simply smiled and nodded at each other before commencing. Taking turns, the two men ruthlessly beat Hawk. His head snapped back several times from the force of their blows, which bloodied his face.

After a few punches around Hawk's eyes, his left one began to swell shut. He could taste blood streaming into his mouth from the growing number of wounds.

With Hawk barely recognizable, the men switched their tactics, concentrating on Hawk's mid-section. They pounded him in the stomach and chest before bashing him on the upper portion of his back that was exposed. Still bound to the chair, Hawk couldn't do anything but brace for blow after blow and hope he managed to survive.

The door opened at the far end of the room, and Fazil strode through.

"What are you doing?" Fazil demanded in Arabic. "I said to beat him up, not kill him."

The two men shrugged and exited with Fazil, who scolded them as they walked away.

The door slammed shut behind them, and Hawk was left alone again with his thoughts in the dark. His face felt like it was on fire. Sweat trickled into the wounds, creating a burning sensation. And there was nothing he could do about it.

In a matter of minutes, Hawk's mood had changed from hope to despair. He wondered if it was even possible to escape—if he even managed to survive the night after the beating he'd just endured.

All Hawk could do was fight to stay alive and pray for a miracle.

CHAPTER 13

Washington, D.C.

NOAH YOUNG NAVIGATED to the address of the website Blunt had mentioned might have live streaming coverage of James Peterson's alleged meeting with a Russian ambassador. At the prescribed time, the image came on his screen and he watched as Peterson entered the room along with his guest. They both took a seat on chairs opposite from one another right near the camera. A faint smile spread across Young's lips as the number of viewers escalated to more than a million within the first thirty seconds.

But that was all Young had to smile about for the next few minutes.

Peterson began his conversation with the ambassador in a congenial manner. The two men discussed their families, and Peterson mentioned how difficult it was on his wife to be traversing the country at so many political rallies.

"But it's worth it," Peterson said. "And she knows that. She wants to make America an even better country and knows I'm the man to help set that in motion."

"I've only spoken with your wife on a couple occasions, but I believe she's right," the ambassador said. "However, I would also add that I think you're also going to be a good leader for the entire world. We need some men like you to restore faith in government."

Young sneered as he witnessed the exchange.

Why don't they just kiss already?

"I appreciate your willingness to speak with me today," the ambassador continued. "As you know, we are behind in some areas of technology, though you will never hear anyone in our government admit that. We are also ahead in other area. Ultimately, I believe we need each other. I know that you have become a successful businessman in your own right, but deep down you are still a technologist at heart. I want to know if you think there are ways our countries can partner together to increase technological platforms all over the world and bring more learning tools to people in less developed nations."

Peterson smiled and nodded knowingly. "This is one area I'm excited about. We need good partners who are committed to making investments in foreign nations so that we level the playing field, so to speak.

I think it's important for someone toiling away in rural Zambia without access to schools to be able to gain an education in some other shape or form. Or even the child in Haiti who can't afford the burdensome cost of school—how will they learn? There are great tools being developed right now that can address some of those issues. We would love to have some nations partner with us on a venture like this. Instead of exporting our brand of democracy to the world through warfare, I'm excited about sharing knowledge in a peaceful manner. This could really bring about the kind of peace the whole world desires right now."

Young felt his stomach sink as Peterson struck the right note in his conversation with the ambassador, one that voters, who had tuned in to watch Peterson fail spectacularly, witnessed in what appeared to be a voyeuristic venture. If this was how Peterson acted in private with foreign dignitaries, he just closed the deal with the American public. According to Blunt, the nature of Peterson's conversation with the Russian ambassador was supposed to be about forging allies to control their respective governments, not a groundbreaking summit. The fact that such a meeting was illegal could be seized upon by Young, but it'd just make him look like a political buffoon in light of how the conversation unfolded. Young sighed and shook his head, unable to deny that his slim chance to direct the narrative of the last few weeks of the campaign had all but vanished.

Then Peterson nearly obliterated every shred of goodwill he'd just engendered in a jarring display of bravado. He shook hands with the ambassador and watched him exit the room before Peterson walked right up to the camera. Looking directly at it, he delivered a fiery message for Young.

"I don't know how many people are watching this live stream, but I suspect it numbers in the hundreds of thousands," Peterson began. "And you all tuned in today because my opponent, Noah Young, worked behind the scenes to set me up. He abused his power and position to navigate the dirty back channel waters of politics to attempt to expose me as some kind of political neophyte orchestrating a sinister plot with our supposed enemies. However, the truth is Noah Young is the one being exposed today as the same old tired bureaucrat that our country has grown tired of, the kind of man who bullies his way to power."

Young's eyes widened as he watched Peterson excoriate him personally in such a public manner.

"Earlier today, officials at the Federal Bureau of Investigation informed me that someone with political ties to Young rigged this very meeting room with hidden cameras in an attempt to live stream what you were all privy to today. But as you can see, this wasn't what was advertised. You likely came here to see me strike some under-the-table deal on terrorism with Russia, but instead you found out the true reason for this meeting—for the betterment of the world.

"And that's what my presidency is going to be about. We're not only going to make America strong, we're going to make the world stronger by doing things that benefit all of humanity instead of just one country. Meanwhile, Noah Young and his campaign will likely deny all this. Their plan is to continue to do more of the same that will leave us more susceptible than ever to terrorist attacks and at the mercy of those who seek to do harm to us all. It's evident we need each other more than ever in the world today, and that's what you're going to get with me.

"Noah Young hoped to expose me as a traitor, but the real traitor is already temporarily sitting in that Oval Office. Let's make sure it's very temporary. I'm James Peterson, and I approve of this message."

The feed went dark.

Young's phone started to buzz with texts from political allies. His secretary buzzed him with calls from his lawyer. He turned on the television in his office to watch the commentators on cable news already offering an instant analysis to what just unfolded in front of millions of Americans.

Young buried his head in his hands as he wondered if there was any way he could possibly spin this into a positive moment for his campaign. And as far as he could see, there wasn't.

CHAPTER 14

Washington, D.C.

BLUNT SHIFTED IN HIS SEAT as he watched Justin Frazier settle into a chair across the table. After serving on the Senate Intelligence Committee, Blunt had spent plenty of time with Frazier poring over reports and discussing policy. They'd also accumulated hours together on Blunt's fishing boat, reeling in large mouth bass and drinking their fair share of beer. With so many memories of good times, Blunt struggled with the fact that Frazier obviously had a hand in Blunt's arrest.

"I wish I could say it was nice to see you, Frazier," Blunt said. "But given the circumstances, I think you'd know I was lying."

"Do you want a lawyer present before we talk?" Frazier asked.

"Do I need one?"

"Depends on how you want to play this?"

Blunt shook his head, still in disbelief. "Does that mean I have a choice?"

Frazier leaned forward, clasping his hands together and resting them on the table.

"Even when we're presented with only one option, there's always a choice. You can decide to go along or resist. It's really up to you. But whatever you choose, there will always be consequences, some good and some bad."

"Cut the bureaucratic crap," Blunt said, punctuating his statement with a grunt. "I know you're the reason I'm sitting here right now."

"And you're the reason I'm the head of the NSA, at least partially the reason. Without you, I don't know if I'd ever have found my way up the ladder in the intelligence community."

"Then how about do your old friend here a solid and get me out of here," Blunt said. "And when you're done with that, go on record with the press to clear my name. It's hard enough fighting all the baseless reporting these days, so an outright statement of my innocence would be most appreciated."

"Unfortunately, that's not how is going to work."

"What's your problem, Frazier? What have I done to piss you off so royally that you'd do this to me?"

"I know this is unsettling for you, but you need to sit back and relax. There are some things at play right now, things bigger than you ever imagined. You just so happened to be the pawn we needed to make the right move."

"So that's what I am to you now? A pawn?"

"Are you listening to me? This isn't really about you."

"It certainly feels that way when you have me handcuffed and perp walked up the front steps of the FBI. Now, why don't you fill me in on this grand plan?"

"I've been instructed not to."

"By whom?"

"I can't say."

"Can't or won't? Which is it?"

"Look, I'm trying to let you know in no uncertain terms that there are some things going on right now that require us to keep you here."

"So am I under arrest or not?"

"For all intents and purposes, you are."

"So this is all for show?"

Frazier nodded. "That's one way of putting it."

"Then you're eventually going to drop the charges, right? Because we both know this is some bullshit."

"I know it might be hard for you to believe right now, J.D., but I am on your side. However, you know what you were doing wasn't exactly legal."

"Let's not get hung up on technicalities here. You run the NSA and should know a thing or two about the blurred lines when it comes to capturing a criminal."

"And if such a situation arises when we need to do something a little above and beyond, we figure out a legal loophole."

"Give me time with my lawyer, and I'll find one, too."

Frazier shook his head. "But that's the thing— we need you here, under arrest by the FBI for what you did. It's the only way."

"The only way for what?"

"J.D., we both want the same thing, that much I know. And I wish I could tell you more, but I'm just not at liberty to do so."

"I've got as much clearance as you do, if not more, by direct permission of the President of the United States."

"This has nothing to do with the president," Frazier said. "You're just going to have to trust me on this one. Know we have the nation's best interest at heart."

"What about *my* best interest?"

"When have you ever been one to elevate your personal interests over the interest of the country?"

"I don't usually, but right now I've got a lot going on and need to be helping. One of my agents is in the Middle East at this very moment on a dangerous op to find out where Al Hasib intends to use the state of the art sea mine weapon they stole from Colton Industries."

"Which agent? Brady Hawk?"

Blunt nodded. "If he doesn't find out where Al Hasib intends to use that weapon, there will be some serious consequences."

"I'm sure Brady Hawk will be able to take care of himself," Frazier said. "From what I understand, he's got a damn good track record."

"But he might need my help."

"*Might.* But we *definitely* need to keep you here if this plan is going to succeed."

"I'm begging you, Frazier, don't keep me in the dark on this."

"I wish I could tell you more, but this is a tight internal operation right now, and you being here is vital for its success. But don't worry—it should be over very soon."

Frazier stood and exited the room without glancing back at Blunt.

Blunt was left to seethe over his treatment and figure out a way to find out what was really going on. Whatever it was, if Frazier was so tight lipped about the operation, Blunt concluded it couldn't be good.

CHAPTER 15

Washington, D.C.

ALEX WATCHED THE LIGHT flicker off the metallic ducts as she steadied her breathing. Her elbow itched, the feeling of fire covered her arm. But she dared not move. Waiting out the prying eyes of at least two FBI agents was a challenge, but she was up to the task, given the dire consequences that would befall her if she got caught. She refused to strand Hawk.

"You see that?" one of the agents asked while his light danced down the duct.

"Where?" asked his colleague.

"Up against the edge there, about halfway down. Do you see it?"

"What is that?"

"It looks like a flash drive of some sort to me."

Alex stayed still. The vent cover creaked as one of the agents swung it open.

"Come to papa," one of the men said.

Alex heard the man's hand sliding down the duct until the sound stopped with a slight knock against the side.

"Would you look at that?" the man said.

"Thumb drive?"

"It would appear so. But it's clever. She disguised it to look like a bullet."

Damn it.

Alex remembered that she'd placed a novelty flash drive that looked like a bullet in her pocket. The device contained the conversation between President Michaels and the fabricated voice of Oliver Ackerman. Resisting the urge to dig into her pocket to confirm her suspicions, she listened to the rest of the agents' conversation.

"What do you think is on it?" one agent asked.

"If this belongs to Alex Duncan, there's no telling. Based on the file I read on her, she's probably seen more state secrets than anyone working at the NSA."

The vent cover creaked as the agents slammed it shut.

"What are you doing?" the other agent asked.

"Our work is done here."

"You don't think she could've crawled inside there?"

The other agent laughed. "She's an analyst and a handler, not an acrobat. No way she climbed up in that duct and shimmied far enough away so we wouldn't find her. Besides, I'm hungry."

"Roger that. Let's get out of here and grab a bite to eat. She'll eventually turn up, if one of our agents downstairs hasn't spotted her already."

Alex held her breath until she heard the door slam shut, the noise reverberating off the walls of the empty room. The apartment was temporary and she'd barely had time to purchase a bed and other essentials, much less furniture for other parts of the home.

Though she let out a sigh of relief, she remained relatively frozen for a half hour before gathering up the nerve to re-enter the apartment. Letting herself down feet first, she pushed open the vent and eased onto the floor. She crept up to the front door and looked through the peephole to see an FBI agent posted outside.

Faced with a new problem, Alex realized she needed to get out of the apartment before more agents returned to scour the place again. She tightened the strap on her laptop bag and headed for the side of the apartment that connected to the fire escape. Before she opened the window, she glanced across the room at the desk where her desktop computer once sat. All that remained were a few stray cords strewn across the floor.

She took a deep breath and eased the window up. Poking her head over the ledge, she tried to identify any agents standing guard nearby. From her first cursory glance, she didn't see any. But that didn't mean there wasn't one lurking below. She had enough experience to know that the homeless man rooting around in the garbage could very well be someone working under cover. But she couldn't wait any longer, especially if she wanted to help Hawk again.

Slipping through the open window and onto the fire escape, she decided to go up instead of down. Taking two steps at a time, she ascended to the roof. She walked up to the edge of all four sides of the building, stooping over just far enough to get a picture of what was happening on the street. As she suspected, the front of the building facing the street was busy, but the alleys were generally clear and presented an easier path to disappearing into the bustle along the sidewalk. After surveying the situation for a couple minutes, Alex concluded the best way to exit the building would be to leap to an adjacent building and leave through the downstairs entrance.

The closest building was no more than six feet apart, but it felt like sixty to Alex. She took a deep breath, backed up along the roof, and broke into a dead sprint. Just as she reached the edge, she jumped—but her foot hit the small cement lip around the perimeter and sucked away her momentum.

Alex let out a squeal when she realized her attempt to make it safely to the other building was in jeopardy. She threw her hands as high as she could before she felt them smack the other ledge. Grabbing on with all her might, she stabilized her body against the side of the building and pulled herself up.

She looked at her hands, which were shaking. Peeking over the edge, she shuddered to think how close she was to a swift fall to her death.

Alex hustled over to the center of the roof and opened the access door. She descended the stairs until she reached the main lobby. As she looked outside, she saw an FBI agent standing outside monitoring the pedestrian traffic. She cursed underneath her breath and sought another way out of the building.

She identified a side exit where residents could dump larger trash. Easing the door open, she stuck her head outside to see if there were any more potential roadblocks to her escape. The coast appeared clear.

Alex decided to utilize the alleyway and head to a parallel street. Just as she was passing the dumpsters, a man clambered out from behind several garbage bags and stumbled after her.

"Hey, Miss," he said, slurring his words. "Could you spare some change?"

Alex ignored him, casting only a suspicious

glance at him as she tightened her grip on her bag strap.

"Hey, I'm talking to you. Can't you help an old man out?"

She glanced back over her shoulder once more and didn't notice the man who'd stepped right in her path. Alex slammed hard into the man.

"Well, what do we have here? A nice little lady like you in a place like this?"

Alex tried to sidestep the man, but he slid in front of her.

"Excuse me," Alex said as she tried to push past him.

Meanwhile, the first man who'd been speaking to her was now just a few feet behind. Alex looked at him again and realized he wasn't so drunk as she initially thought—it was all an act.

"I don't want any trouble," she said, attempting to get past the man once more.

"Neither do we," the man in front of her said.

"What's in the bag?" the other man asked.

Alex pursed her lips and darted to the left and then back right, eluding the man's grasp. She pumped her arms and ran as fast as she could, knowing her best chance was to make it to the street before they caught her.

She thought her plan would work—right up until

the moment one of the men caught her from behind, tackling her onto the ground.

Alex hit her head hard but didn't lose consciousness. However, she did lose her grip on her bag, which was quickly snatched up by one of the thieves.

"Don't be so stingy next time," the other man said. "A little bit of kindness goes a long way."

The two men hustled off as Alex was left to deal with the scrapes and bruises she'd sustained. She felt fortunate they didn't harm her any more physically. But the laptop was gone—and with it, her chances of helping Hawk dwindled.

CHAPTER 16

Iraq, undisclosed location

THE SECOND ROUND of beatings Hawk took weren't quite as vicious as the first, but the comparison would've been meaningless to most people. Hawk had been tortured before, even by Al Hasib goons, yet this time felt different. As he remained tied to a chair, he wondered how the body had so many pain receptors. He didn't want to pass out again, but he felt that was inevitable.

Hawk awoke some time later, unsure of whether it had been minutes or hours. But it was just in time to receive yet another beating. Two men loomed over Hawk and traded turns walloping him. Body blows, kicks, roundhouse punches—fists and feet collided with Hawk at a torrid pace. He finally fell backward in his chair as the men mercifully decided they were done. Hawk's face was drenched, though he couldn't tell whether it was sweat or blood before concluding it was likely a healthy mixture of both.

I just might die this time.

Hawk resisted the urge to accept his fate. He understood his limitations and realized he couldn't survive another attack. If he didn't escape before the tag team torturers returned, his fight against Al Hasib would end at their hands.

A half hour passed before the door opened again.

Hawk moaned. "Can't you just wait a little longer this time?"

"Excuse me, Mr. Hawk," the man said in English. "I'm just here to bring you some food and water."

There was something about the man's voice that sounded familiar, though Hawk was unable to identify anyone with any certainty due to the dim lighting and his swollen eye. Hawk craned his neck toward the direction of the door, wincing with pain as he did.

"I'm gonna have a helluva time trying to eat with my hands tied up like this."

The man eased across the floor and set a tray down at Hawk's feet. "Relax, Mr. Hawk. I'm here to help you."

Hawk squinted, searching his memory banks for the name of the man. "Do I know you?"

"Indeed. It was quite some time ago, but given your state, it's understandable you don't remember me."

Hawk's memory kicked in. "Kejal? Is that you?"

"I apologize for underestimating you, Mr. Hawk."

"You've learned English?"

"Uncle Jaziri taught it to me before I joined Al Hasib."

Hawk smiled and sat upright in his chair as Kejal began untying the bindings.

"Your uncle is a good man."

"Allah rest his soul," Kejal said.

"He's dead?"

"Someone in Al Hasib killed him."

"Then why are you . . ." Hawk's voice trailed off, answering his own question before he finished asking it.

"Revenge, of course," Kejal said. "I was more or less forced to join, but I decided to find out who pulled the trigger and killed Jaziri. He was such a good man, especially to me. I never wanted any of this. I just wanted to herd my goats and be left alone."

"Yet, here you are."

"As are you—but not for long."

Hawk felt the rope fall from his wrists. He rubbed them and turned around in his chair to face Kejal. "Are you going to help me get out?"

Kejal nodded.

"They'll kill you, you know."

"That's why you're going to beat me up before you leave," Kejal said.

"I can't do that."

"You must or, like you said, they will kill me."

"Kejal, come on."

"I won't take no for an answer, but before we do that, I need to tell you a few things."

Hawk stood. "Go on."

"First, I want to thank you for returning my bike in one piece. I was very angry, but I know why you did what you did. As a result of being with you on the mountain that day, I began to see the world in a new light. That's when Uncle Jaziri began not only teaching me English but also educating me on the evils of Al Hasib and other groups like them. I'm not sure what would've happened to me if you hadn't gone with me to tend my herd."

"That's kind of you to say, but your uncle is the one who deserves all the credit," Hawk said. "He was a good man and I'm saddened to hear of his passing."

"He was a very good man. He would also want me to help you, which is why I'm here. Al Hasib has stolen a weapon, which is why I imagine you're here."

Hawk nodded. "It wasn't that difficult to figure out, was it?"

Kejal flashed a faint smile. "If you plan to stop them from using it, you need to go to the Strait of Hormuz."

"I was afraid of that."

"They are going to target oil tankers and create chaos with the markets."

"That's their goal?"

Kejal shrugged. "I'm not sure. I hear whispers when I get into meetings, information I'm sure Fazil or any of the leaders wouldn't want someone as lowly as me to hear. But I've heard them nevertheless."

"And you're sure about this?"

"A team of several men was dispatched there two days ago to deploy the weapon. I'm not sure when they plan to start firing it, but the results will be disastrous."

"And Fazil has no other plans?"

"I can't be certain of anything else. I don't have the clearance to attend such meetings. I just glean what I can from listening to the men talk. But Fazil always seems to be planning something, and there's been talk of something really big. Maybe this attack in the Strait of Hormuz is what they were talking about."

"Thanks, Kejal. I only need to know one more thing."

"What's that?"

"How do I get out of here without being seen? Given my current state, I don't think I would fare well if I had to engage any guards."

Kejal gave Hawk an escape route as well as the keys to one of Al Hasib's vehicles located in the garage.

"Take my keffiyeh, and make sure to wrap this scarf around your mouth," Kejal said as he handed the scarf to Hawk along with a card. "Show this access card to the guard at the gate, and they shouldn't give you any problems. And don't forget your pack in the corner."

Hawk patted Kejal on the shoulder. "Your uncle would be proud of the man you've become. Good luck on your mission to avenge your uncle's death. I wish I could talk you out of it though."

"No one will be able to do such a thing."

Hawk slung his bag over his shoulder and turned to leave before Kejal called out.

"You're forgetting something," Kejal said.

Hawk turned around to see Kejal pointing to his face.

"Can't we do this another way?" Hawk asked.

"No, we—"

Hawk delivered a wicked blow before Kejal finished responding, knocking him out cold.

"You're a good kid," Hawk said. "I hope you stay alive."

He threw Kejal's keffiyeh on and entered the hallway to make an escape.

CHAPTER 17

Washington, D.C.

NOAH YOUNG WANTED TO CANCEL all his campaign appearances for the next couple of days to avoid the onslaught of questions sure to be directed toward him by a frothing media. The sudden death of President Michaels had caused a firestorm of coverage, not to mention the endless chatter on the airwaves about the looming constitutional crisis. But Congress quelled the furor by delaying the election for a month—and the media had now found a new story to latch onto. The kind of attention that accompanied such a controversy was not what Young needed if he was going to upset Peterson, who'd emerged as the frontrunner.

Young's campaign manager, Blake Mayfield, quashed any ideas of slipping into the shadows and waiting out the media's maelstrom regarding

Peterson's accusation shown live on the Internet and since replayed thousands of times on every news program in America.

"How do you think it's going to look if you cancel now?" Mayfield asked. "You're going to look guilty as sin."

"If the shoe fits . . ."

"Wait. You didn't—" Mayfield said before stopping himself. "Never mind. I don't want to know. I need at least some shred of plausible deniability."

"Look, everyone knows Peterson is a snake in the grass. His defense plan is to make friends with everyone, let them plunder what's left of our country, and move us toward some one world order. And that's the last thing we need right now."

Mayfield removed his glasses and rubbed his eyes. "*That's* the message we need to be selling right now, not turning tail and waiting it out. Let's go on the offensive, instead of staying in a defensive posture."

"I'm not sure how well that will play with the American people."

Mayfield shrugged. "I'm not sure we have any other choice. Peterson is a political veteran. He knows how to destroy his opponents to gain power. It's his *modus operandi* if you study all his previous election campaigns."

"And has anyone tried the tactic you're suggesting?"

"Not successfully, but—"

"Perhaps we need to strike a different tune then."

"I disagree. Everyone else who has fought back against Peterson when he wanted them to hide tried to do it using scandals and dirt. You're going to hit back by outlining the truth regarding the policy he'd implement if he were to win. That will speak volumes to voters, not only about what kind of man Peterson is but also what kind of man you are. *Noah Young isn't the kind of man who stoops to his opponent's level and slings mud—he's a man of action and cares about his country. He's a patriot.* That's the kind of message you want to send."

"That's also the truth."

"We've got that working for us then, which is more than we can say for Peterson, isn't it?"

"You know what Peterson and that Russian ambassador were really going to talk about today? They were going to—"

Mayfield plugged his ears. "Lalalalala. I don't want to hear it. Plausible deniability, remember?"

Young stopped. "Fine. I want to tell someone the truth."

The door swung open and Young's chief of staff, Hal Knightley, stepped inside.

"Why don't you tell the truth to the feds since they're here to speak with you?" Knightley said without skipping a beat.

"Were you listening outside?" Mayfield asked.

Knightley shook his head. "No, but I heard what the president just said before I stepped inside."

"Why don't you knock next time like a polite politician?" Mayfield snapped.

"Polite politician?" Knightley said with a chuckle. "You haven't been around Washington very long, have you?"

"Cut it out," Young said. "This is serious. The feds are really here to speak with me?"

Knightly nodded. "They arrived about fifteen minutes ago and are requesting an interview immediately."

"Tell them they'll have to wait," Young said. "I'm not ready to speak with them."

"I don't know about that," Mayfield said. "If word gets leaked out that you refused to speak to them—"

"Someone is going to start a rumor no matter what you do," Knightley said. "If you're not comfortable speaking with them right now, tell them to go take a hike. They work for you anyway."

"The FBI's top brass is all loyal to Michaels," Young began. "I think they still blame me or see me as somehow responsible for his death."

"That's something they need to get over," Knightley said.

"Not if they're going to use it against Noah just to destroy his campaign," Mayfield said. "All it takes is one source whispering something to a *Washington Post* reporter and it's going to be taken as the gospel truth by most Americans. Any chance at nuance is lost once they begin that game."

"That's par for the course in Washington politics," Knightley said. "We all know that. So, I'm just asking what difference does it make if he wants to take some time to think about it and develop a strategy with all his advisers? This is a critical point in the campaign. If we make the wrong move, it'll be over before you can say *President Peterson*."

"And I think the wrong move would be to put off the FBI and give anyone there with a grudge an opportunity to torpedo the campaign," Mayfield said.

Knightley put his hands on his hips. "Well, Mr. President, you're in charge. It's your campaign. But if I were you, I would tell them to stick it in their ear. You're running the country and don't have time for petty accusations like the one Peterson brought today on the Internet. For all we know, he set that up himself just to bring you down."

Young sighed and shook his head. He stood and paced around the office, mumbling to himself.

"Does he always do this?" Mayfield asked.

"Get used to it," Knightley said. "I'm not sure if

he's speaking with the ghost of Lincoln or the spirits that are simply tormenting him. But he talks to them all the time."

Young glared at Knightley. "This is how I like to process things. Do you have a problem with it?"

Knightley looked wide-eyed at Young. "Whatever works for you. It's your thing."

"I need to make a call," Young said. He sat down at his desk and dialed his secretary. "Can you get me General Van Fortner on the line?"

"Certainly, Mr. President," she said.

A few seconds later, Van Fortner answered the phone.

"Mr. President, how are you?"

"I've had better days, though lately there haven't been many good ones."

"Are you catching a lot of flack for that stunt Peterson pulled?"

"So, it looked like a stunt to you?" Young asked.

"What else could it have been? Like you would've authorized any such spying on Peterson. That's just ludicrous. And it's not like he could prove it anyway."

Young didn't say a word.

"Mr. President, are you still there?"

"Still here, General," Young said. "Are you aware that the FBI arrested J.D. Blunt and have accused him of orchestrating that whole debacle with Peterson?"

"That's absurd. I've known J.D. forever, and I know he does a lot of crazy stuff, but he'd never do something like that on his own volition. If he did it, someone with a lot of sway put him up to it."

"Look, I didn't call you to talk about that," Young said. "I wanted to ask you what you think I should do right now. The FBI wants to speak with me, and I haven't even talked with my lawyer yet. How bad do you think it will look if I tell them to forget it?"

"I'd wait and speak with more of your advisors," Fortner said. "You can never be too careful in cases like these. The implications of what a conversation with them will mean could dramatically impact the election—for good or for bad. You just don't know what it'll be. And not speaking to them will also have a similar effect. But if you engage in a conversation with them, at least you can control the narrative."

"Good point, General."

"Now, if it backfires on you, please don't hold me accountable."

"Okay, I'll grant you immunity if that's the case," Young said.

"Excellent," Fortner said with a nervous laugh. "Now I can sleep with a clear conscience tonight, knowing I'm not going to be tossed in federal prison for any bad advice that I gave the president."

"I appreciate your perspective, too."

"Any time, Mr. President," Fortner said before he hung up.

Young froze. With bulged eyes and a furrowed brow, he stared at Knightley.

"What is it, sir?" Knightley asked.

"I just heard a click on the line right before I hung up."

"You've never heard that before?" Knightley asked.

"Someone was listening in on my call, weren't they?"

Knightley nodded. "See. What did I tell you?"

Young seethed as he glared at Mayfield. "Go tell the FBI that I need more time."

CHAPTER 18

Washington, D.C.

BLUNT TOSSED AND TURNED all night as he slept on the hard cot one of the FBI agents had brought into the interrogation room. At the first glint of sunshine trickling through the blinds, Blunt got up, ready to put the night behind him and face a new day. He wanted to hear news that whatever secret operation was underway would have occurred overnight and that he could be released.

An agent knocked on the door, gaining Blunt's permission before placing a cup of black coffee on the table and slipping out into hallway.

"Didn't I already tell these jackwads I don't drink coffee?" Blunt groused before dropping the cup into the trash. He then yelled, "A real breakfast would be nice."

A half hour passed before Justin Frazier entered the room.

"How'd you sleep?" Frazier asked.

"You owe me big time after this," Blunt said, his voice gravely. "I've had better nights sleeping on the dirt during combat."

"In that case, I've got sort of a good news-bad news scenario for you," Frazier began. "Which do you want to hear first?"

"Might as well give me the good news since none of the news I ever get from the intelligence community is truly good news."

"Tonight, you're going to get to sleep on a real bed."

Blunt eyed Frazier closely. "And the bad news?"

"It's going to be at one of our safe houses."

"Damn it, Justin. A safe house? Really? What the hell is going on that you have to keep me detained for another night?"

"The truth is, we don't know how long we're going to need to keep you."

"This is ridiculous. Just let me go home and keep me under surveillance there."

"Too many loose lips around this place," Frazier said. "Of course, if this was at the NSA, I could trust everyone to do the right thing and keep their mouths shut. But this is the FBI, and this place has become so politicized that I don't want to risk blowing this thing apart."

"Can't you at least tell me what's going on?"

"I wish I could, I really do. But we're keeping this operation on a strict need-to-know basis only in order to protect against any leaks."

"I think I have a right to know what's going on," Blunt said as he narrowed his eyes. "You know I have the clearance for it."

"You also know I could arrest you for what you did."

"I'd like to see you prove it. Now, I want my lawyer."

"You're not getting a lawyer, J.D. You're here on your own accord so we can help catch a criminal who is attempting to sabotage this country. Now, I've said more than I should have already, but that's all you're going to get out of me. In an hour, an FBI agent will escort you to a safe house where you'll stay for the duration of this op. Is that understood?"

"If we ever go fishing again, I just might feed you to the sharks," Blunt said with a growl.

"Did you get your morning coffee?" Frazier said before hitting his forehead with his index finger. "Oh, that's right. You don't drink coffee. You're just this grumpy no matter what time of day it is."

Blunt pointed at the cot. "You'd be grumpy, too, if you had to sleep on that damn thing all night. I thought for sure you were preparing me for an interrogation this morning."

Frazier smiled and shook his head. "You never

change, do you, J.D.?"

"My need for sleep has never changed, nor has my hatred for coffee," Blunt said. "And last night I got no sleep, and some green-behind-the-ears agent dropped off a steaming hot cup of coffee first thing this morning after I told them I don't drink the stuff."

"Perhaps I can schedule a massage at the safe house for you. Would you also like a mani-pedi?"

"I don't know what the hell a mani-pedi is, but I hope you choke on it."

"It's not a drink," Frazier said. "It's a—oh, never mind."

Blunt watched Frazier leave the room and disappear down the hallway. Desperate to get out of the FBI offices, Blunt eased up to the door and jiggled the handle. It was locked.

"Those punks are imprisoning me," Blunt muttered to himself.

He proceeded to sit down on the cot, burying his head in his hands.

* * *

AN HOUR LATER, Blunt was led out the back of the FBI headquarters in a black SUV. The two agents assigned to watch him asked questions that signaled they had no idea who he was. After a few minutes, Blunt stopped their get-to-know-you inquisition.

"How old are you guys?" Blunt asked.

One man was thirty, while the other was twenty-eight.

"And you seriously don't know who I am?" Blunt asked. "Haven't you watched the news?"

"Wait a minute," one of the agents said, snapping his fingers. "Weren't you that senator who faked his death? I think I do remember this story now."

Blunt sighed. "Yeah, that was me."

"Why'd you do it?" the other agent asked. "I'm always curious why people want to disappear. Was it for love? For money? Or were you running from something?"

Blunt chuckled. "Certainly wasn't for the first two. I've got plenty of money and my first love is this country."

"Then you were running from something?" one of the agents said.

"Yes, I was. Ironically enough, I was trying to escape from a very powerful person in this country."

"Next you're going to tell us that it was the president," the other agent said as he laughed.

Blunt didn't laugh with him, remaining stoic.

The agent covered his mouth with his hand. "It was the president. Oh my god. What happened?"

"There are some things I just prefer not to relive," Blunt said.

When they finally arrived at the safe house, Blunt

retreated immediately to his room and announced he was taking a nap. After a restless hour of sleep, he wandered into the living room and turned on the television.

"I don't think that's a good idea," one of the agents said as he tried to take the remote control from Blunt's hand.

"I'm bored as hell, and I'm not going to sit around and do Sudoku puzzles for the next however many days despite how subtle the suggestion is made in my room by the dozen Sudoku books piled on my nightstand."

"But there are some things on television you probably don't want to see."

"If you're worried about my feelings, don't be," Blunt said. "I've seen enough fabricated stories about me to last several lifetimes. And I'm immune to it all. I've never been one to be bothered by another person's opinion about me."

"Fair enough," the agent said, releasing his hand from the remote. "Just don't come crying to me when Anderson Cooper starts saying mean things about you on television."

Blunt settled down onto the couch and turned on the television. He flipped through the channels until he came across a mid-afternoon cable news program where a fiery debate was underway about the election. Then a question flashed up on the screen: Will Blunt's Arrest Sink Young's Election Hopes?

Blunt watched as the pundits sparred verbally over the impact of his arrest and how it was effecting polling numbers. None of the discussion was encouraging to Blunt, and even more devastating to Young's hopes of staying in the White House.

One of the agents leaned against the doorjamb leading into the living room.

"See, I told you that you wouldn't wanna watch this."

Blunt felt sick to his stomach. Whatever had transpired over the past twenty-four hours while he was held up in the FBI headquarters wasn't good for him or for Young's campaign.

Blunt felt the urge to get out of there and do something about it—and fast.

CHAPTER 19

ALEX DIDN'T HAVE TIME to grab her go bag before the FBI agents had stormed her apartment. All that she was left to survive with was the money she'd crammed into her pocket as she attempted to keep all the incriminating evidence hidden. She knew she could likely talk her way out of anything and get Blunt to help her out by pulling a few strings, but there wasn't time to plead her case and explain the urgency behind her actions. Hawk was in danger, and she needed to help him—only now she couldn't. Without a computer and thousands of miles away, Alex was left to scramble for help and hope that she'd still be able to make contact with Hawk once she was back up and running.

Following her beat down in the alley, she trudged to the street corner and caught a cab ride to a seedy motel on the edge of the city limits. Washington was pricey, but there were still a few places with cheap motels, though not the kind she ever wanted to frequent. But she had no choice.

She barely slept the night before, subjected to raucous noises from the room next door. After the third set of couples took up residence at 4:00 a.m., she questioned whether the place was actually a motel. She finally managed to get a long stretch of sleep between 5:00 and 8:30 a.m. before housekeeping rapped on her door.

"Come back later," Alex said with a groan.

"Sorry, toots," the cleaning lady said. "Time's up. Check out is at 8:00 a.m. for the rate you paid."

Alex walked over to the door and cracked it open. "I'm going to get another day then. Come back later."

"No can do, lady. Boss man's orders."

"Fine," Alex said before stumbling out of the room and purchasing another night.

When she returned, she found the room barely cleaned. Her bed was still messy, and nothing had been thoroughly wiped down.

Alex stepped back outside and called out toward the woman. "You call this clean?"

"Maybe you shouldn't have made such a big mess," the lady replied. "Besides, you wanted me to come back later anyway."

Alex sighed and retreated inside her room. She

HARD TARGET | 147

took a shower, hoping it would clear her head. She needed to get back online but required the kind of help she couldn't afford at the moment. While she was washing her hair, she remembered that she still had one ally she could reach out to who just might be able to help.

If anybody can help me, Mallory Kauffman can.

Due to her fugitive status, Alex was reticent to involve Mallory. But Alex was desperate. Hawk was flying solo in the middle of the desert, yet she had no idea what was happening with him or if he was even still there. If he needed her help, she didn't know it.

Once Alex got dressed and straightened up her room, she called Mallory.

"Long time, no see," Mallory said as she answered the phone.

"These days, the *no see* is kind of the point," Alex said.

"Trouble always seems to follow you, doesn't it? What's the problem this time?"

"I'm not sure I want to get into it over the phone, but I do have a problem that I think you can help me out with."

"Tell me what you need, and I'll see what I can do."

"Some punks stole my laptop yesterday, and I need to get it back."

"Of course," Mallory said. "Not sure I can help you with that though."

"It's not that complicated. I just need you to look up the location on a website for me and go with me to that place and get my computer back."

"If it's that easy, why do you need my help?"

Alex sighed, unsure of how much to divulge on the phone. "Look, I don't want to get you in mixed up in the middle of all this, and I wouldn't unless it was absolutely necessary."

"So, it's absolutely necessary."

"Let's just say at the moment that I don't have access to any computer, nor do I have enough money to do so."

"You need to fill me in," Mallory said. "Give me the website address and your current location, and I'll come pick you up."

Alex shared the information with Mallory and waited for a few moments while she looked up everything.

"What are you doing staying at the Beltway Motel? I've heard stories about that place."

"Trust me," Alex said. "They're all true. If you've ever heard about a senator coming here, just know they are either working with an organized crime group or hiring a hooker."

"Classy place, huh?"

"You'll see it for yourself when you pick me up."

"Can't wait," Mallory said. "And, oh, I've got a hit on your laptop tracker. It's still active. It's in a shady part of town too. You sure you don't want to call someone else?"

"Just bring your gun and your badge. We'll manage."

"Be there in half an hour."

Alex hung up and waited. She imagined the worst when it came to what happened to her computer: The punks who stole it stripped it clean—or worse. She wondered if they'd already reformatted the hard drive. Both were nightmare scenarios.

When Mallory knocked on the door, Alex hesitated before opening it. Her situation was an utter embarrassment, especially for someone who used to have a dream job at the CIA. Instead, she was holed up in a sketchy motel in a questionable part of town, reaching out for help regarding a situation she was uncomfortable talking about on the phone. Alex took a deep breath and forced a smile before turning the deadbolt.

Mallory smiled and gave Alex a friendly hug. After they both stepped back, Mallory scanned the room.

"What have you gotten yourself into this time, Alex?"

"I know it might seem strange, but I can explain."

"Why don't you tell me on the way," Mallory suggested. "I don't want to stay here any longer than we have to."

"Fine by me."

Mallory clicked her key fob. Alex eased inside and buckled her seat belt. She waited patiently for Mallory to do the same before explaining the events that led to the laptop theft.

"That's quite a story," Mallory said. "How much longer can you go before you run out of cash?"

"Tonight," Alex said. "I'm paid up through tonight, and then I'm out of cash."

"Go grab your things," Mallory said. "You're staying with me until this thing gets sorted out."

"I really don't want to drag you into this, Mal."

"Too late. I'm here, and I don't care what you want. I'm going to help you. Friends don't let friends stay at the Beltway Motel, even if it is for only one more night. Besides, where were you going to go after this anyway? A friend's couch? The street?"

Alex didn't say anything.

"You were planning on staying on the street, weren't you?" Mallory said. She pointed at the room door. "Go get your bag now."

Alex hustled inside and scooped up scant belongings before shoving them into her bag. She returned shortly to Mallory's running car.

"I'm going to take care of you," Mallory said as she drove out of the parking lot and in the direction of the laptop's tracker. "Whatever is really going on here, I'm sure we can sort it out. I've just never known anyone who finds herself in such predicaments on a regular basis."

"Believe me when I say this, but I wish it wasn't that way."

"Pining for your old job as a CIA analyst, are you?"

"Not exactly," Alex said. "I wouldn't trade this job for the world. I just . . ."

"Just what, Alex?"

"I just wish a different group of people supported it."

"You mean like the government?"

"Yeah. Just not some shadowy organization that constantly seems to be at odds with those in the intelligence community."

"Well, I've got an office full of people who would gladly trade places with you. There's not a day goes by when we all wish we were in your shoes, including me."

"Even after you saw the situation I'm in now?"

"It's still much better than the ham-fisted bureaucratic mess we have to deal with. As much as the Beltway Motel is a human-sized roach trap, it's still worlds better than navigating all the red tape and over-inflated egos we have to endure daily."

"Would you still feel the same way if I told you the cleaning lady yelled at me this morning and called me 'Toots?'"

"Still more pleasant than getting groped on a regular basis by one of your superiors and ogled by the most recent divorced agent."

"I guess you have a point," Alex said.

"And besides, you get to work with Brady Hawk. It can't be all *that* bad."

"I'm not gonna lie. He's about the nicest eye candy around."

Mallory cast a sideways glance at her passenger. "Is that *all* he is? Just some eye candy?"

"I'm not ready to predict anything right now. But I will say things are moving in the right direction."

"I knew it," Mallory said, pumping her fist and smiling. "That guy is crazy good looking. I thought you'd be a fool if you didn't break protocol and entertain the idea of a relationship with him."

"It won't come to much of anything if I can't get my laptop back so I can help him."

"That bad, huh?"

Alex nodded. "We'd uncovered one of Al Hasib's hideouts, and he was about to break into the compound when my satellite feed went out. The coms followed shortly thereafter. And this was all a few minutes before the FBI stormed into my apartment."

"Well, we're almost there," Mallory said. "Just let me handle this for you, okay? It's the least I can do."

"You're a life saver, Mal. I appreciate you sticking your neck out like this for me."

"You know I'm always down for your crazy adventures. Beats looking at numbers and listening to phone calls all day."

A few minutes later, Mallory slowed down as she checked the address. "Looks like we're here."

They both got out of the car and strode toward the apartment.

"Will your tracker tell us which floor they're on?" Mallory asked, glancing at her phone.

"No," Alex said, "but I can set off an alarm. There are only three floors here, so I'll go up to the second floor and you stay here on the ground. Select the alert function and listen. We should be able to tell which one it is."

"Sounds easy enough."

Alex hustled up a flight of stairs before signaling to Mallory to activate the alert. It went off for five seconds before Alex motioned for Mallory to join her.

"It's up here," Alex said.

Mallory hustled up the steps and pounded on the door with her fist.

"Who is it?" a man asked.

"Mallory Kauffman from the CIA. I need you to open up now."

"Do you have a warrant?"

"I don't need a warrant," Mallory said. "I'm going to give you to the count of three to open this door. Otherwise, I'm coming in."

Alex heard some rustling in the house and fleeting footsteps. "They're headed out the back."

Alex raced down the steps and around the building where one of the men was preparing to leap to the ground. He was focused on his leap and never saw Alex.

The moment the man hit the ground, Alex kicked him in the face. He rolled to his left and felt the corner of his mouth for blood. Once he stood, he narrowed his eyes and glared at Alex.

"Oh, you're gonna pay for that," he said as he started to rush toward her.

Mallory clicked off her safety, her gun trained on the man's back.

"I wouldn't do that if I were you," she said.

The man turned around and noticed Mallory.

"Who are you people?" he asked.

"We're just here to retrieve some stolen property," Mallory said. "Now I suggest you hand that nice young lady the laptop in your backpack before I pump some lead into you. Think you can go along with that deal?"

The man didn't say a word, seething as he dug through his bag and fished out Alex's laptop. He handed it to her.

"Is that it?" Mallory asked.

Alex turned it on and stared at the screen as she waited for it to come to life. The computer whirred, and the login window appeared.

"This is it," Alex said.

"Good," Mallory said before looking directly at the man. "You got off easy today. If I as much hear you breathe a word of this to anyone, I'll send an army of DEA agents over here and they'll have your sorry ass in jail for the twenty years. You understand?"

"Lady, I don't even do drugs," he said. "I just—"

"Just what? Hustle vulnerable women in dark alleys? I think that's even worse. But don't you worry. Whatever charges come your way will most definitely stick."

"I'll stop, lady. Just point that thing elsewhere," he said, gesturing toward Mallory's gun.

She lowered her weapon and eyed him closely.

"I suggest you get on out of here and find a respectable means of employment."

He nodded and dashed off down the sidewalk.

Alex smiled. "You may have just turned that man's life around right there."

Mallory rolled her eyes. "He'll be locked up before the end of the week. The only things he regrets right now are that he got caught and he got kicked in the face by a woman. I doubt either of those things will score him many points with his gang."

"Well, let's get out of here before we draw any attention," Alex said. "I need to find out where Hawk is and if he needs my help."

Alex looked down at her comlink as it started to blink.

"What's that all about?" Mallory asked, gesturing toward the device.

"Someone's online," Alex said as she inserted the earpiece. "It's Hawk."

CHAPTER 20

HAWK BUMPED ALONG THE ROCKY ROAD in the truck that he'd stolen from Al Hasib. He shoved in his earpiece and had fallen into a rhythm of trying to raise Alex on the coms every five minutes or so without much luck. But he persisted and was rewarded when Alex finally answered him after a couple of hours.

"Are you okay?" Hawk asked.

"I should be asking you that question," Alex answered.

"Since you weren't responding, I figured something had to have happened to you. It's not like you to leave me stranded in the middle of a mission."

"Well, your suspicions are correct. Something did happen to me, but I don't want to get into it right now. Tell me how you are and how I can help."

"I'm alive," Hawk said. "And currently, I'm speeding along one of these godforsaken Iraqi highways headed for a port so I can get to the Strait of Hormuz."

"Did you get captured?"

"Captured, tortured, and questioned."

"And released?"

"Not exactly," Hawk said. "Fazil left me alive because he said he wanted me to watch him bring the world to its knees. Then I learned that the weapons system is going to be utilized in the Strait of Hormuz. It's going to cripple the world's oil prices and give Al Hasib control if they manage to commandeer any boats as they hold all these tankers hostage."

"How'd you escape?"

"It's a long story, but the short version is that I had some help by a nice young man who's infiltrated Al Hasib to take revenge for the death of his uncle."

"So, what can I do for you?"

"Meet me in Oman," Hawk said. "I need you on site with me if we're going to disable the weapon. This is one mission I can't do on my own. I need your savvy tech skills to snuff out this threat."

"And you're sure that's where the weapon is going?"

"I'd bet my life on it," Hawk said.

"How exactly are we going to disarm it? Do you have a plan?"

"I'm still working on that, but I'll have it all figured out by the time you get here."

"Are you sure we'll have enough time before Al Hasib starts using it?"

"I don't know. But I do know we don't have much time, so do whatever you can to get to Oman. I'll send you the exact location for where we can meet up."

"Be careful, Hawk."

"You know me."

Hawk hung up and continued on his route toward Um Qasr, a port city a stone's throw from Kuwait. After stopping for gas in Basrah, Hawk purchased a first aid kit to clean up his face as well as a cell phone. He bandaged himself up before he called Thomas Colton to learn more about the best way to disarm the underwater weapon.

"Hello, Son—I mean, Brady," Colton said as he answered the phone.

"It's been long enough since you found out the truth. You need to stop calling me that."

"Old habits die hard."

"So does your habit of letting terrorists get their hands on your weapons."

"And I'm hoping that you'll be able to stop them. Is that what this call is about?"

Hawk sighed. "Sort of. I need to talk with one of your top technical experts to learn about the weapon's vulnerabilities and what the best is way to shut it down."

"Then you'd want to speak with Dr. Carl Morton, the head of our research and development team," Colton said. "Carl conceived the design for the mine weapons system and will know if there are any easy ways to disarm it. Let me patch you through to him—and good luck."

"Thanks," Hawk said.

He waited as the line started ringing again.

"This is Dr. Morton."

"Hello, Dr. Morton, this is Brady Hawk, and I'm the one who's trying to retrieve your mining system that was stolen recently from Colton Industries by Al Hasib agents."

"Nice to make your acquaintance on the phone, Mr. Hawk. I've heard plenty of stories about you."

"Don't believe everything you hear, Doc. But I didn't call to chat about the exaggerated stories people tell about me. More to the point, I was wondering if you could walk me through how I could disable the device, especially if it's something I can do from a fair distance."

Morton sighed. "Unfortunately, if you want to disable the weapon, you'll need to be on site to do it."

"In other words, if it's already underwater, I'm going to have to dive down to shut it off?"

"Precisely. I thought placing the kill switch on the torpedo launcher would be a good way to avoid the enemy being able to render it useless if they didn't know where it was located."

"You didn't even consider what might happen if they decided to use it themselves?"

"I know, I know," Morton said. "It was a huge error in judgment, but there's nothing I can do about it in this particular situation."

"You're probably not aware of this, but Al Hasib intends to deploy the weapon in the Strait of Hormuz if they haven't already, the shipping lane for more than seventeen million barrels of oil each day."

"Oh, my. What have I done?"

"Listen, Doc. Anything useful you can tell me that would help me locate the device quickly would be helpful. The Strait of Hormuz is quite vast in size."

"Well, there is one fail safe I included in the event that the currents moved the weapon and made it more difficult to find."

"Go on."

"On the operating console, there's a button that will set off a homing beacon that will go off under-water. You should be able to hear it if you dive beneath the surface with any type of listening device."

"What if I can't get access to the console?" Hawk asked. "Trying to get access to the console is going to add another degree of difficulty to my mission that I'm just not sure I have time for."

"It operates on a wireless signal," Morton said. "If you're savvy enough with a computer, you could potentially hack into the console and set off the homing beacon."

"I know a person who can do that for me."

"Good. Just tell me where to send the instructions for gaining access to the back end."

Hawk gave Morton an email address.

"Now for the big question," Hawk said. "How do I shut down the weapon once I locate it."

Morton laughed nervously. "Believe it or not, that's the easiest part. There's a chip you can remove that would render the device inoperable. You certainly won't be able to raise it to the surface without some heavy equipment."

"Right now, we just want to stifle any threats. We'll worry about salvaging anything later."

"Fair enough. I'll include a diagram of the launching mechanism and instructions on how to remove the chip in my email."

"Thanks, Doc."

"No, thank you, Hawk. I'm praying you're successful in your endeavor."

"Pray hard," Hawk said. "This isn't going to be easy."

Hawk hung up and groaned softly. The mission had seemed challenging before, but the degree of difficulty just increased significantly upon learning the only way to shut down the weapon. The only thing that gave him a little bit of confidence was the fact that he had his Navy Seal training to rely on now.

If anyone could do this, Hawk could. And he knew it—but that was little solace given the consequences should he fail.

CHAPTER 21

Washington, D.C.

NOAH YOUNG ADJUSTED HIS TIE and took a sip of water before preparing to look over the speech handed to him by one of his writers. With the rumor mill run amok, Young felt the need to use what little power afforded to him as the fill-in president to get his message out, bypassing all the news filters. He wanted the voters to hear for themselves what was really important about the election. James Peterson was not going to direct the national conversation if Young had any say in it.

Blake Mayfield approached Young's desk several minutes before the speech was set to air.

"You don't have to do this," Mayfield said. "We can come up with a reason why you had to postpone."

Young looked up at Mayfield. "Do you still think this is a bad idea?"

"It's not the worst idea I've ever heard of, but I don't think you stand to gain much by going on television right now and trying to deflect. The people are going to want answers to the questions Peterson raised. And if you don't answer them, they are going to draw their own conclusions. Letting people decide for themselves what actually happened is not the best move right now."

"Peterson can raise all the questions he wants, but what voters really want are answers to the issues that affect their everyday lives. If they feel safe and secure, they're going to have little to complain about. People with extra change in their pocket rarely raise an uproar."

"And is that what you think the people care about?"

"That's what every person from the beginning of time has cared about," Young said. "It's a universal truth."

"In more recent times, people have also cared about whether or not their politician is honest. That's why Peterson's questions have to be addressed or else people are going to assume he's right."

"Sorry, Blake. You're my campaign adviser, not my campaign nanny. And right now, I'm going to head off in a different direction on this issue. I usually agree with you, but not in this instance."

"I'm pleading with you to do this. I don't want to see your whole campaign torpedoed over some insinuation that is patently false."

Young shook his head. "I won't do it."

"Won't? Or can't?"

Young cleared his throat and glared at Mayfield. "If you'll excuse me, I need to finish prepping for this speech."

For the next ten minutes, Young read and re-read each line on the page. He wanted to keep his remarks brief in order to ensure that the entire clip was able to be shown on the news. He'd thought through everything, even as his campaign manager begged him to cancel the talk.

Young received a signal from one of the White House techs that they were ready to go live in thirty seconds. At ten seconds, a countdown began, and before Young could blink, he gazed at the camera and began.

"My fellow Americans, I come to you today not in an effort to defend myself from the reckless and baseless accusations hurled at me by another candidate, but instead to reassure your faith in the government and the plan in place that has been working for the last four years. President Michaels was beloved far and wide for his winsome personality, even if his policies weren't always embraced by politicians on both sides of the aisle. Nevertheless, his vision for America was one that I share—and one that I think you share, too.

"Just like the late president, I have a dream to see America become safe and prosperous, a place where freedom in every sense of the word reigns supreme. And while some candidates might choose to use terrorism as a political football and attempt to score points with voters, I refuse to do that. Instead, I want to issue a challenge to our entire nation today, one that we must all embrace if we're ever going to see the end of terrorism and end more senseless tragedy: Republicans, Democrats, Libertarians, and every other political stripe in between, let's work together to create policies that deter terrorists and systems that help us catch those still emboldened enough to commit such an act against innocent Americans.

"In closing, I want to remind us all that as citizens of the greatest country in the world, we all have a duty to be the best we can be for the betterment of those around us. It is with that heart that I accepted the emergency nomination to allow the process of democracy to smoothly move forward in this nation. I do not chase power for power's sake, but only for the chance to be a leader in healing the long-standing divisions we've endured and to encourage us all to find joint solutions. Thank you for your time."

Young nodded at the camera and held his gaze until the camera man gave him the signal that the feed had been cut. With a long sigh, Young threw his head back against his chair and slumped. He closed his eyes and went over every word in his mind. All he could do was hope his intuition was right and that Mayfield's suggestion was wrong.

"Good job, Mr. President," Mayfield said.

Young opened his eyes and looked to his right at a scowling Mayfield.

"You're saying one thing, but your face says something entirely different."

Mayfield looked down at his feet. "I've got some bad news, quite damning actually, especially in light of what you just said about Peterson's *reckless and baseless accusations*."

"Out with it, Baker. You're not writing a click-bait headline here."

"I just received a call that *The New York Times* is running a story tomorrow about two men who supposedly conspired to remove President Michaels from office and that his death wasn't really an accident as previously reported."

"Who on earth is feeding them such garbage?" Young asked.

"The only silver lining in all of this is that you aren't named or implicated in the article," Mayfield said. "But I think it's fair to say many people will draw their own conclusions about who those two men are and what role you played in it. After all, you were at Camp David when Michaels died."

"What do you want, Baker? Would you like for me to take a polygraph test and prove to everyone that I'm not lying?"

"That'd be a start."

Young glowered at Mayfield. "It's a damn shame when your own campaign manager doesn't trust you."

"That's my point, sir. If I don't believe you, who will?"

"I have half a mind to fire you right now," Young bellowed. "Now get out of here before I change my mind and actually go through with it."

Young watched Mayfield scamper away. If there was one thing Young appreciated in his staff, it was people who weren't afraid to challenge him. But Mayfield was pushing the limit on what was acceptable. His actions didn't quite fit the definition of insubordination, but he was questioning the integrity of his candidate, which was something Young didn't appreciate or have much patience for.

Mayfield stopped at the door and turned around. "One more thing, sir."

"What is it?" Young said.

"I placed the latest poll numbers on your desk.

With just over three weeks to go before Election Day, you're now trailing by ten points nationally in the latest conglomerate poll."

Young picked up the report and scanned it. His real crime was attempting to expose Peterson to the American people before it was too late. But nothing was working. He needed a political victory to stop the bleeding and possibly boost his support.

And he needed that win yesterday.

CHAPTER 22

BLUNT WATCHED A REPLAY of Noah Young's comments to the nation on one of the cable news stations and shook his head. Despite Young's attempt to squelch the scandal before it blew up, Blunt recognized the truth for what it was: a failed attempt to redirect the election toward issues. With a past full of successful campaigns, Blunt recognized long ago that nobody really cared about the issues. Winning an election was all about how people felt about you when they went to the polls. An apathetic feeling would doom a candidate just as much as a negative one would. And with less than a month before the election, independent and undecided voters had a good feeling about James Peterson and were anywhere from negative to on the fence when it came to Noah Young.

"I think I'm going to call it a night, maybe read some before I go to bed," Blunt announced to the FBI agent charged with guarding him in the safe house.

But Blunt had other plans.

He went into his room and came out about fifteen minutes later.

"Is it me or is it hot in here?" Blunt asked as he trudged down the hall. "Can we turn the heat off?"

The agent turned around and glared at Blunt. "It's only thirty-six degrees outside. Are you insane?"

"Maybe I'm just having hot flashes."

"Are you going through menopause, too?"

"Watch it," Blunt said. "Forget it. I'll just crack my window."

"You do that, Senator," the agent said as he turned back around and refocused on the television.

Idiot.

Blunt strung together a couple of the bed sheets and tied one end off at the headboard post. He flung the rest of the sheets outside. With his cane in his mouth, he eased his way onto the ground. After shoving the sheets back inside, Blunt started for the road. He considered calling a car with Uber but decided that would be a fast way to get recaptured. If he could reach Young somehow, Blunt figured the president could help him at least wait out the pending legal matter until it was resolved. Anything but being holed up in an FBI safe house.

Blunt had almost reached the road when he heard one of the agents call after him.

"You're not going to get very far, Senator," the agent said.

"Then you're going to have shoot me," Blunt said as he continued walking toward the road.

The agent hustled across the yard toward Blunt, who picked up his pace. Just as the agent reached Blunt, he spun around and delivered a vicious blow with his cane that knocked the man off his feet. Blunt didn't stop to revel in his direct hit, instead turning forward and continuing on.

The agent scrambled to his feet as another agent rushed outside to help his partner.

"This isn't going to end well," the agent said.

Blunt threw his hand up in the air dismissively and kept walking.

"Okay, it's your choice," the agent said.

As he neared Blunt, the statesman whirled around with his cane only to have it met by a firm hand.

"I wasn't born that long ago, but it wasn't yesterday," the agent said as he tightened his grip on Blunt's cane and snatched it from his hand. "Now, come with us."

The two agents led Blunt back into the house and ushered him onto the couch.

"Stay there while I call my supervisor," one of the agents said as he slipped into the hallway.

After a conversation conducted in hushed tone, the agent returned to the room.

"I have good news for you, Senator. Justin Frazier is on his way over here and is going to speak with you about everything that's going on."

Blunt glared at the men. "Can I go to my room?"

The agents both looked at each other and chuckled. "I think you've lost that privilege for now. I'll also be setting the alarm just in case you become hot again and get any ideas about opening your window."

* * *

BLUNT WAS STILL SEATED on the couch with arms crossed when Justin Frazier entered the safe house. He lugged a small briefcase with him, hoisting it onto the kitchen table before saying a word. Flipping the latches with his thumbs, Frazier opened the case and pulled out a host of file folders, stacking them with precision.

"Well, J.D., you certainly know how to get what you want," Frazier said.

Blunt grunted. "If that were the case, we wouldn't be here talking right now."

"I mean, you want to know what's going on and the real reason behind why you're here, so I'm going to tell you—sort of."

"Sort of? What the hell kind of explanation is that going to be?"

"Come over here, and I'll tell you."

Blunt stood and lumbered over to the kitchen seat, pulling out a chair directly across from Frazier. The two men sat down, and Frazier took the first portfolio off the top and sifted through several papers.

"How long is this going to take?" Blunt asked.

"I can't let you see all this, but I'm—"

"Why the hell not? I've probably got a higher security clearance than you do."

"I'm going to let you see a few documents, though some of the names have been redacted. Given your current ties to the White House, I thought it was best not to divulge everything. Eventually it'll all make sense, but in the meantime, I'll share what I can, which should clear up the muddy waters for you."

"If it can get me out of this dump of a safe house any faster, I'll be all ears."

Frazier held up his hands. "Look, this isn't some prerequisite for your release. This is a courtesy to you."

"You just want to keep me from trying to run off again, don't you? You think placating me will keep me more content."

Frazier shrugged. "I'm hoping so, though your last get away attempt didn't get you too far. It's just that I have a lot of respect for you and what you've done, both professionally and as your friend. I don't want to leave you in the dark."

"Fine. I'll listen—and stay put . . . for now."

"Okay, here's what's happening in a nut shell. The NSA teamed up with the FBI on a high-profile case to capture a high-ranking official in Peterson's campaign who is working with foreign terrorists."

"What? James Peterson? Mr. Anti-Terrorism Man?"

"The one and only," Frazier said. "And now perhaps you see the problem we have. The FBI didn't want to see this investigation publicized for fear of being unable to capture the suspect in the act. But even more so, the FBI didn't want to take heat for politicizing an investigation. They learned from the last time."

"Seems smart, but I don't understand why I'm being supposedly arrested. My good name and reputation is at stake."

"We'll clear all of that up after this is over. I think the American people will be understanding—even though what you did was still wrong. The truth is we set you up to be a patsy."

"You *sonofabitch*," Blunt said with a growl.

"One of my analysts came to me with an opportunity, suggesting we use you unknowingly in this op."

"What if it hadn't worked?"

Frazier smiled. "We knew it would work the whole time, but there were other backup plans in place just in case something went sideways. We certainly weren't anticipating the show that Peterson put on though, that's for sure."

"Now when you say *working with terrorists*, what exactly do you mean by that?"

Frazier took a deep breath and then exhaled slowly. "Well, at this point, all we know is that this person of interest has contacted a liaison from Al Hasib. The plan is to sneak one of their operatives into the country very soon to work with a sleeper cell."

"Do you know where they plan to strike or what they plan to do?"

"Nothing yet. We're still gathering more intelligence, but we know something is going to happen very soon."

"How soon?"

"Maybe within the next week or so. It's going to happen before the election, which I think is the point."

"That bastard Peterson wants to invite an attack just before everyone goes to the polls to assure a victory. What an idiot. He's already steamrolling Young, if the polls are to be believed."

"It seems like overkill to me, too," Frazier said. "But maybe Peterson is making a plan to loosen the defense purse strings when he gets into office. He does have quite a number of big financiers in the tech industry given his background. I'm sure they're all hoping he sends a few contracts their way."

"Or maybe he just wants to make sure he doesn't choke like he did in that California senate race about a decade ago when he blew a fifteen point lead with a week to go and vowed to never enter politics again."

"Whatever his reasoning, we need to stop him before this attack comes to fruition and hundreds of innocent Americans die."

"And arresting me helps you how?"

"There have been whispers going around the Beltway for a while now about a joint venture between the NSA and FBI to arrest a high-profile political figure," Frazier said. "This will quell those rumors and hopefully make our target more comfortable than he should be. Perhaps he'll make a mistake and we'll be able to catch him."

Blunt leaned forward in his chair, signaling his full interest in the situation. "You need to be proactive on this," Blunt said. "Sitting back and hoping someone will make a mistake is a good way to watch another tragedy occur."

"I didn't mean to imply that we're not actively pursuing the target, just that we're still gathering the intelligence we need to make an arrest."

"Arresting him is the last thing you need to be concerned with if what you think is going to happen will occur. You need to stop the threat first and foremost. Worry about compiling enough evidence to put him away in federal prison later."

"That's not how we work, J.D. You ought to know that by now."

Blunt sighed. "Don't I know that all too well. It's why you have to have people like me to do the dirty work. We may not always operate within the confines of the law, but we snuff out threats and save lives, all while protecting the good name of the United States of America to the world abroad."

"And we appreciate what you've done, but we're going to handle this one our way," Frazier said as he started to place the folders back in his briefcase.

"I need to make a phone call," Blunt announced as he stood.

"I'm sorry, but I can't let you do that."

"This is important, Justin. If you don't let me do this, those innocent people you're so concerned with just might die like you fear."

"We're already on it. You don't need to worry about it."

Blunt narrowed his eyes and pointed at Frazier. "No, you don't understand. You and your little army of eavesdroppers aren't going to be able to stop what's about to happen."

"We're sticking with our plan. Injecting any other players into it endangers our success."

"Success is making sure there aren't body parts splattered all over a city street. Now, if you'll let me make a phone call, I'll get someone here who can put your mind at ease and catch this terrorist scum. What's really going on here? I have a feeling you're not telling me everything."

Frazier sighed. "Okay, I wasn't be completely straight forward with you."

Blunt sat back down. "What is it, Justin?"

"We have reason to believe that the terrorist is actually already here in the country. More precisely, we believe he's already in New York planning his attack."

"In that case, you really do need me to make this phone call."

"Who are you so desperate to reach?"

"Brady Hawk."

"And where is this Mr. Brady Hawk?"

"Since you're finally being completely honest with me, I might as well tell you the truth—I have no idea where he is."

"In that case, Mr. Hawk won't do us much good, will he? Just leave it to us. You do your part by staying put so we can ferret out the rat."

Blunt nodded, but he wasn't in agreement.

CHAPTER 23

Kumzar, Oman

HAWK HELD ALEX'S HAIR BACK as she leaned over the side of the boat. The combination of a rich meal the night before and choppy waters led to an upset stomach that could only be solved one way. When she finished puking, Hawk handed her a towel followed by a bottle of water. She thanked him before easing into her seat and hoping the worst was over.

A half hour later, the captain slowed the boat down and eased into the fledgling port of Kumzar. The northernmost settlement in Oman happened to be located on an island at the edge of the Strait of Hormuz. The captain explained to Hawk and Alex that the people were generally friendly and welcoming to tourists.

"But we're not tourists," Alex said to Hawk in a whisper.

"If we say or do anything that would show otherwise, be prepared to go under the microscope," Hawk said. "And I doubt you're prepared for Kumzari curiosity. It's a special breed from what I hear."

"We'll make sure to keep a low profile," Hawk said. "We're honeymooners, right?"

"If that's the case, where's my ring?"

Hawk reached into his bag and produced a fake diamond ring.

Alex's mouth fell agape. "Hawk, what is *this*?"

"If we're going to look the part, we need all the right props."

"Hmm. Nice prop."

"It's a fake, Alex. Now, should we go over the plan again?"

She shook her head and adjusted the ring on her finger. "I think I've got it. You just need to get me close enough to hack into the console so I can set off the homing beacon. Should be easy enough. You're the one with the hardest job, not me."

"I hope you're wrong about that."

The captain docked the boat and helped them get out. Hawk thanked the man and slipped him an extra hundred dollar bill to get Alex roses for their room. He winked at the man and gestured toward the ring on her finger. The captain smiled and nodded knowingly.

Hawk and Alex proceeded to check into their hotel room, which was located on a rocky cliff overlooking the harbor. He set up all his reconnaissance equipment and scanned the area below for any signs of Fazil's men.

"Are you seeing anything yet?" Alex asked after ten minutes of silent searching.

"Nothing so far. There's plenty of activity around the docks, but nothing that looks suspicious at the moment. Mostly just fishing and tourism boats."

Another five minutes passed without a word spoken between either of them.

Hawk stood. "I need to go down there and scope it out."

"Right now?"

He nodded. "It's just before lunch. By the time I get down there, the place should clear out a little bit, and maybe I'll be able to get a better feel for what I need to do to get you close enough to hack into the system."

"From the report you gave me, I only need to be about fifty meters away. That should be close enough for me to gain access to the network."

"Any chance beyond that distance?"

She shook her head. "It's a localized system, and the back entrance is designed to latch on to any cellular networks in the area. However, the only way you can gain access is through a special bluetooth portal the engineer created. It's a boosted bluetooth signal, and fifty meters should be strong enough for our needs. All I need to do is engage the homing beacon. I could be done in less than a minute if everything goes as planned."

Hawk shot her a sideways glance. "Nothing ever goes as planned."

"You don't have to tell me that, but a girl can dream, can't she?"

"*Realistically*, how long will it take?"

"Maybe five minutes tops," she said. "That should allow for any extra hiccups I might encounter."

"Fair enough. That at least lets me know what I'm dealing with in getting you close to the boat."

"What makes you think Al Hasib even has the control panel on one of their boats here?"

"It's too heavy to lug around. Plus if someone decided to, it'd likely draw quite a bit of unwanted attention. At least, that's what Kejal told me."

"Good luck down there," Alex said. "I'll keep an eye on you from here. What's your cover going to be?"

"I'm going to ask if any of the tourism boats know of a spot where we can cliff dive around here. I've always dreamed of doing something like that on my honeymoon."

Alex laughed softly. "For some reason that doesn't surprise me."

"Yeah, I'm not the kind of guy who will just grab a book and read by the beach for the entire vacation. I need to be doing *something* active."

"You might try relaxing sometime," she said. "It can be therapeutic."

"The most therapeutic thing I can do right now is put an end to this threat in the Strait of Hormuz. Maybe after that, I'll consider a lazy vacation with you."

"In that case, I've got a list of places we could go to waste the time away."

Hawk wagged his finger. "Don't get too excited. We need to stay focused and finish this assignment first."

"Good luck," she said.

With his pack slung over his back, Hawk made his way down to the docks to scout out the area and look for the potential boat that contained the control system. The biggest problem Hawk had was that almost all of the boats appeared rather modest without much room to house such a device. The larger vessels were prone to attract attention in a small harbor such as the one on Kumzar, and Fazil was smart enough not to make a mistake like that.

Where are you, Al Hasib?

Hawk stopped and spoke with a boat captain about the possibility of hiring him later that afternoon for a tour around the island. Trying to remain as casual as possible, Hawk continued scanning the area for a likely candidate. When nothing stuck out to him, he left the harbor area and walked along the shoreline for a couple miles. Finally, something caught Hawk's eye.

Anchored just off shore at an inlet away from the main docks was a boat that looked out of place. At about forty feet in length, the craft had sleeping quarters below deck visible by way of several porthole windows. One man stood at the helm hunched over. Hawk noticed the man had a gun holstered as he stood upright and began walking around the deck. As he strode about, he looked off in the distance, but there were no lines of concern etched into his forehead. Hawk figured the guard must have thought everything was as it was supposed to be and didn't give much more than a cursory glance at the shoreline.

Hawk hid behind a row of trees just off the shore. With the tide going out, the boat was in shallow enough water that Hawk noted he wouldn't have to swim far once he decided to approach the vessel.

"Hawk, how are things going?" Alex asked. "I'm looking through the binoculars, and I don't see you down at the harbor? Are you still there?"

"I had to look elsewhere," he said. "Couldn't find anything, but I think I stumbled upon something now just west of the harbor."

"What do you see?"

"A boat anchored in a secluded inlet that doesn't belong with one armed guard moseying around the top deck."

"Don't just rush in there, Hawk. I don't have eyes on you."

"It shouldn't be a problem. I only see one guard."

"Stay where you are. I'm coming down there."

"Roger that."

Hawk hunched low in the bushes, eyeing the guard. But after five minutes, Hawk was convinced the man was alone. Waiting for Alex would just complicate things.

I'll have this taken care of before she gets here.

Hawk eased farther down the beachhead until he found an ideal location to enter the water. After he was submerged, he swam up to the boat and waited for the right moment.

As Hawk clung to the boat's step ladder, he went over how he would handle the guard. Without a gun due to the water approach, Hawk needed to make quick work of the man patrolling the deck and take his weapon. Hawk thought if he could handle everything without a shot being fired, he would be in good shape to inspect the vessel and locate the control panel. But that was all conditional upon everything going as planned.

A few minutes later, the guard lit a cigarette and strode aimlessly around the ship. At one point, he stooped over the railing and glanced downward yet never laid eyes on Hawk who was near the back of the ship. Hawk seized the opportunity to make a surprise attack, presumably with the guard's back turned.

Scampering up the ladder, Hawk raced toward the Al Hasib guard, who had just started to turn toward the noise of heavy footfalls. But he never even saw Hawk's face. Hawk slit the man's throat and eased his body down onto the deck. Taking the man's gun, Hawk headed below in search of the control console.

The click of a gun froze Hawk.

He held his hands up and turned toward the sound.

"I thought we were alone," Hawk said, scanning the cabin for any other guards.

The Al Hasib agent kept his eyes and gun trained on Hawk but yelled something in Arabic that Hawk didn't understand.

Another man called out something to the guard, who scowled and screamed back another slew of words Hawk figured was some sort of code talk.

As the back and forth banter continued, the guard glanced away from Hawk for just a second. But that was all Hawk needed.

With a roundhouse kick, he sent the guard staggering backward. A throat punch followed and then another slit of the throat.

How many more of there are you?

Hawk surmised there was at least one other guard based on the conversation that had occurred just moments before. But making assumptions could get him killed. He'd already made a dangerous one before engaging the Al Hasib operatives on the boat without Alex to help, and he'd be lucky to escape with his life, which had become a far greater priority than the weapons system control panel.

Hawk dragged the man's body to the corner of the room and then eased up against the wall near the entrance, waiting for the next guard to enter.

Another guard called out for his colleague.

"Mohammed, where'd you go?" he said in Arabic.

Those were also the last words the man uttered.

Hawk hid up against the wall and waited for the next man to walk into the room. The second he did, Hawk forced a knife into the side of the man's knee. But instead of going for the kill, Hawk punched the man in the stomach and sent him reeling backward. Two more swift punches to the face knocked him down.

"What do you want?" the man asked in English.

"I want to know where the control panel is for your new weapons system," Hawk said, waving a gun in the man's face. "If you help me find it, I'll consider letting you live. But that's all you get at this point. Understand?"

The man nodded and started to say something before a bullet ripped through the back of his head. Another man strode into the room, his gun already trained on Hawk.

"He was going to talk," the guard said. "And I could not allow that."

"I'll make the same offer to you as I made to him," Hawk said. "If you tell me where the control panel is, I'll let you live."

The guard smiled. "Mr. Hawk, you are in no position to make any such deals. Perhaps I should remind you that all I have to do to end this conversation is squeeze the trigger."

"This offer will expire at the end of one minute, at which time I will kill you," Hawk said.

The man laughed but never took his eyes off Hawk. "You are a funny man, Mr. Hawk."

"You know my name. I'm impressed."

"When Karif Fazil is looking for you, everyone knows what you look like."

"So, are you going to take me up on my offer?" Hawk asked.

"It wouldn't matter if I wanted to or not. The weapons system control panel is destroyed—but not before putting the device on auto-pilot. The only way it can be turned off is by going to the actual weapon itself buried fifty meters underwater." The guard looked Hawk up and down before continuing. "But not that *you'll* ever find it in the Strait of Hormuz."

Hawk pursed his lips. "So you're going to shoot me now?"

"Of course not. I'm going to make you suffer just as I was instructed to do."

"And how exactly do you plan to do that?"

"I'm going to make you watch Al Hasib bring your country to its knees."

"Those are awfully bold words coming from a man who's about to die," Hawk said. "You're not even going to be able to make good on that promise."

"It won't be nearly as difficult as you—"

A bullet whistled through the cabin and sunk into the guard's temple. He crumpled to the floor and dropped his gun.

"And you were saying what?" Hawk asked as he stood over the guard's lifeless body.

Hawk looked up to see Alex stride into the room.

"What do you think you're doing?" she asked, glaring at Hawk.

"I saw an opportunity—and I took it," he said. "Nice shot, by the way."

"That nice shot probably saved your life. I had

to kill another guard on deck. And from the body count I've seen so far, that means there were five Al Hasib guards roaming around this place. And you decided to come aboard alone and take them on by yourself? Without backup?"

"I made an unfortunate miscalculation. But fortunately, you assisted me here."

"You call that an assist? That was more like I saved your life."

"And I appreciate that," Hawk said. "But I've got some even worse news on top of everything that just happened here."

Alex narrowed her eyes and cocked her head to one side. "And what's that?"

"The weapons system is on auto-pilot. And there is no control panel."

"Where is the launcher?"

"Underwater," Hawk said as he looked at the guard's body. "And I was just about to get this nice young gentleman to tell me where it was before you killed him."

Alex threw her hands in the air. "Like I was supposed to know that? He had a gun pointed at you—and he didn't look like a man who was about to tell you anything other than something rather impolite."

"I guess we'll never know now, will we?"

"A *thank you* would've been nice."

"Well, I do appreciate what you did, but you realize the kind of predicament we're in now, don't you?"

She nodded. "You would've had a difficult time finding the weapon if you were dead."

"Good point. But we need to get out of here quickly before someone sees us and thinks we're terrorists."

They both ascended the steps leading to the deck. Hawk slid down the ladder into the water first and waited for Alex.

She started to climb down before she stopped. "We really shouldn't leave this boat right here, should we? I mean, we could just vanish into the Caribbean with her."

Hawk shrugged. "If oil tankers weren't about to be blown apart a few miles from here, I might consider it."

She gave him a coy wink. "It was a joke, Hawk. Besides, this ship is rigged with a tracking system."

"How can you be so sure?"

"I already checked," she said before sliding down into the water.

They both slogged the rest of the way onto shore when a man called out to them.

"Well, this is great," Hawk muttered. "Now we'll be the prime suspects on this tiny island."

"Excuse me," the man said in perfect English. "I

was wondering if I could be of any service to you."

Unable to place his accent, Hawk took a forth-right approach with the stranger, who wore traditional Omani garb and a dark splotchy excuse for a beard.

"Are you American?" Hawk asked.

"Hmm," the man said, cocking his head and raising his index finger. "I'd consider myself more of an opportunist."

"What kind of opportunity do you see here?" Alex asked.

"I see two people who might be in need of some information," he said.

"And you're the one who can provide it?" Hawk asked.

"For the right price, of course."

"Of course," Alex said. "Now, let's get down to business."

The stranger winked at her. "I love a woman who's not shy about stating her intentions."

"Then you must not be from around here," Hawk said. "What's your name?"

"My name is Abid—and just because I don't look like I'm from around here doesn't mean that I'm not."

"Nobody from around here likes strong women," Hawk said.

"You'd be surprised," Abid said as he wagged his finger. "But let's not waste any more time on this idle conversation. I'm here to help you."

"In that case, what did you know about the men on this boat?"

"I knew they were members of a terrorist group, likely Al Hasib based on some of the conversations I had with some of them."

Alex's eyes widened. "You spoke with those men?"

"I did more than that," Abid said. "I took them out to sea."

"Do you remember where?" Hawk asked. "It's quite important."

"I gathered that from the size of the machine they needed me to lower into the water for them."

"And you have the coordinates for where you dropped them off?" Hawk asked.

Abid nodded. "For the right price, of course."

"We can give you five thousand dollars," Alex said.

Abid scowled and shook his head. "Have a wonderful day. I must be on my way." He turned and walked back down the path for a few steps before Alex called after him.

"Eight thousand," she said.

Abid looked over his shoulder at her and shook his head.

"We've only got ten thousand," Hawk said. "But

I'm sure someone else would love to take our money. Chances are there are other people around here who knew where you anchored that weapons system."

"I'll take it, though I must tell you it's way below market price for such information," Abid said. "However, at the moment, I am desperate. I was coming to get my money, though I wasn't entirely sure they'd have it. I'd already been blown off once before."

"Let me guess," Hawk said. "They promised you a large pay day, and you took them without getting at least part of your payment?"

Abid nodded.

"You should simply count yourself lucky to be alive," Alex said.

"Perhaps you just saved my life," Abid said. "I was coming down here to demand payment."

"Your compensation may have been in the form of three bullets—two to the chest and one to the head," Hawk said.

"I could unknowingly owe you my life, which is why I've decided to accept the paltry sum you offered."

Hawk pulled out some of the money stacks and waved them at Abid.

"When can we get started?" he asked.

"When would you like to begin?" Abid responded.

"The sooner the better," Alex said.

"I'll begin to prepare my ship," Abid said.

"Where are you staying? The Shati Albahr Inn?"

Alex and Hawk nodded.

"Meet me on *The Marlin* in an hour down at the harbor," Abid said. "We'll leave promptly then."

Hawk nodded. "We will be there."

CHAPTER 24

New York City

KARIF FAZIL CLASPED HIS HANDS behind his back as he climbed the steps leading to the makeshift stage his men cobbled together earlier that morning. The abandoned warehouse Fazil purchased under a shell corporation he'd set up several years ago was on the edge of Manhattan. Its location provided the ideal hub from which to launch the most deadly attack on American soil in the country's history. And Fazil could hardly wait to get started.

Perched on Fazil's shoulder, Jafar squawked to break the silence. Muted chuckles spread among the 300 men standing on the ground. With identical white dress shirts and dark suits, trimmed with dark ties and fedoras, the men all sported Guy Fawkes masks and held black suitcases.

"I want to begin by letting you know what an

honor it is to know that there are this many men living in this godforsaken country who believe this much in our jihad," Fazil said. "Your sacrifice is not viewed lightly, for none of us know what will become in the days ahead. But this exercise is vital for us to carry out this attack and for it to be successful.

"As we have fought hard against the infidels and their blatant disregard for our faith, the number of *fedayeens* who have served admirably for Al Hasib has been too many. If we're going to fight the Americans and emerge victorious, we need all of our best men working together. That's not to diminish the sacrifices already made by our martyrs, but it's important we make every effort to stay alive. Our numbers are small, and every loss hurts more than it does our enemies. We must change that through remaining one step ahead of them and showing them that our resolve is steadfast and our faith in Allah—and one another—will not be shaken."

The men broke out into a chant of "Al Hasib, Al Hasib," their words echoing off the walls. Fazil raised his hands to quell the shouts.

"For our plan to work, each one of you must stick to your route along the streets of New York," Fazil said as he continued. "You cannot deviate in any way or else you could jeopardize the success of the entire mission. You might think you're insignificant because there are so many men here, but you were invited to participate because we think you believe deeply in the vision of Al Hasib. Failure is not an option—and I promise you we will experience the glory of victory if you follow the simple instructions provided to each of you in your briefcase.

"In the morning, we will hold a trial run, and everyone must participate. However, leave your attire and briefcases at home. We must not tip our hand. The Americans are anticipating some sort of attack, and we cannot give them any reason to suspect one is going to happen so soon. The element of surprise is on our side at the moment, and they will not have any idea how we were able to pull this off in the aftermath. However, we know the arrogance of the Americans is what will ultimately cost them. They've never seen the likes of what we will deliver on their doorstep later this week."

Another round of "Al Hasib, Al Hasib" chants broke out before Fazil lifted his right hand, gesturing for the men to be quiet.

"Let's give the city of New York a Veteran's Day parade they'll never forget."

The chanting resumed without any objection from Fazil. He smiled as he looked out across the sea of masks. Jafar squawked again, rustling his feathers and bouncing lightly on Fazil's shoulders

"Don't you worry," Fazil said, rubbing Jafar's head. "You'll get to see it all."

CHAPTER 25

Kumzar, Oman

HAWK CRAMMED HIS GEAR into his pack and secured it as he prepared to leave for the docks. The hotel where he and Alex were staying qualified as modest accommodations, especially for a supposed honeymoon trip. But the location of the Shati Albahr Inn made up for anything it lacked in amenities. Despite the setting, Hawk didn't want to spend another night there.

"Are you sure this is a good idea?" Alex asked.

"Do we have a choice at this point?" Hawk replied.

"It's just that this Abid guy admitted he was an opportunist. We know that's not his real name. His accent is so faked."

"Can't fault a man for trying to make some fast cash."

"I'm just hoping we're the highest bidder."

Hawk pulled her close and kissed her on top of her head.

"That it?" she said, pushing him away playfully. "A peck on the head."

"I'll be back later," he said with a wink. "Maybe we can discuss advancing our relationship."

"A kiss on the lips is first base," she said. "You're still in the on deck circle with that."

Hawk threw his pack down and grabbed her, swooping her to the side and leaning over for a long kiss.

"Is that more to your liking?" he asked as he raised her up.

She smiled and brushed her hair out of her face. "Not a bad start. Now just make sure you get home in one piece."

"You'll be in my ear the whole time," he said.

She forced a smile. "Until you go underwater for the most dangerous part of your assignment."

"Just get packed up so we can get out of here as soon as I'm back. And this time, we're going to fly out of here—I've already made arrangements with a local pilot."

"You didn't want to hold my hair back again while I puked over the side of a boat, did you?"

Hawk shook his head. "It's not your best look."

She smiled. "You sure you don't want me to go with you?"

Hawk shook his head emphatically. "Absolutely not. Too much could go wrong out there. If something should happen to me, I don't want you getting caught up in the middle of it."

"Fair enough," she said. "I'll be ready to bolt when you return."

"Great. See you soon."

She grabbed him once more and kissed him on the cheek. "For good luck."

Hawk smiled and shut the door, hustling downstairs until he reached the ground level. Glancing around, he didn't notice anything suspicious about the people nearby. By all appearances, life on Kumzar was carrying on as usual.

Hawk checked his watch as he strode up to *The Marlin* exactly one hour later after he'd met Abid. Hawk didn't want to admit it to Alex, but he shared her apprehension regarding the self-admitted opportunist. Reaching behind his back, Hawk felt for his gun, just in case.

Abid emerged from the deck below with a smile on his face, arms spread wide.

"Welcome, my friend," Abid said, kissing Hawk on both sides of his cheek.

Hawk pulled back abruptly and glared at Abid.

"I don't do that thing. Americans shake hands."

"I'm not an American."

"You sure as hell sound like one with that fake accent," Hawk said. "But your secret is safe with me."

Abid adjusted his keffiyeh as his eyes widened. "Why don't we just get started? Do you have the money?"

Hawk nodded and stepped aboard. Setting his pack down, he pulled out an envelope and handed it to Abid.

"Ten thousand U.S. dollars, just like we agreed," Hawk said.

Abid peeked inside and inspected the cash. "Looks like it's all here."

"My word is my bond," Hawk said. "Now, let's get going. I don't want to linger in the harbor any longer than we have to. I have work to do."

Abid nodded. "Very well then."

He signaled for his deck hand to untie the boat and shove off. Abid assumed the position behind the captain's wheel and activated the bilge pump.

"You've already been out today?" Hawk said as he watched water spew out of the side of the boat.

"I spend most of my day on the water. You happened to catch me on dry land for the first time since earlier today."

"And you're just now using the bilge pump?"

"Just a habit. Nothing you should concern your-self with."

Hawk shrugged. "How far is it going to take us to get out to the coordinates?"

Abid punched in some coordinates on his GPS and waited a few seconds. "The GPS says it'll take about a half an hour."

"That's right on the edge of the shipping lane," Hawk said. "Seems kind of lazy to me."

"They were in a hurry, and I wouldn't exactly de-scribe them as professionals."

"How'd they get the weapon in the water?"

"Weapon?" Abid said. "I don't know anything about a weapon."

Hawk sighed. "I'm assuming you were hired be-cause this boat has a crane on it and can lift heavy equipment. They dropped what was essentially a tor-pedo launcher into the water. Don't tell me that you didn't notice it."

"Whatever they brought aboard was crated up that day. I didn't look at it, so I could honestly say I have no idea what they want me to drop in the water. They handled everything else."

"Did your crane operator see anything?" Hawk asked.

"I'm sure he did, but he isn't here—and he didn't talk about it afterward."

"You really would do anything for money, would-n't you?"

"A man has to eat and feed his family."

Hawk eyed Abid cautiously. "You don't strike me as the family man kind of guy."

"Looks can be deceiving."

Once the ship cleared the no wake zone, Abid throttled the engine as the boat started to skip across the sea. Hawk watched the sea spray kick into the air, creating a constant mist around the edge of the deck. He inserted his earpiece and tried to reach Alex.

"Are you there, Alex?" he asked.

"I'm here, and you're coming in loud and clear."

"Good. And while I wish you were here, I'm sure you'll be glad that you didn't come along," Hawk said. "This ride is bumpier than our one to Kumzar."

"In that case, I'm happy to hold down the fort."

"Stand by," Hawk said. "We should arrive in less than half an hour."

"That's not very far out into the Strait of Hor-muz."

"That's what I said, but Abid acted like he didn't know anything about what the Al Hasib agents did. And if he did, he's not talking about it."

"I knew there was something sketchy about that guy."

"Nothing we can do about it now. He seemed

pleased to get the cash and is driving me out to sea."

"Hopefully not to just shoot you and dump your body."

"I'll be ready if he tries to pull such a stunt."

As the ship cruised along, Hawk reviewed the protocol for disabling the torpedo launcher. The directions he'd been given seemed straightforward, but he didn't have any margin for error. He needed to be sure he knew every step in the protocol. By the time he finished, the boat bounced as it slowed.

"Almost there," Abid called to Hawk.

Hawk nodded and put on his wet suit. By the time he was dressed appropriately, Abid sauntered down to the main deck.

"This is where we anchored," Abid said. "How long should we plan on you being down there?"

"Not long. What's the depth here?"

"It's about fifty meters, give or take a few. You should be fine in your suit."

Hawk checked his oxygen tanks once more before securing them on his back. He put on his flippers.

"See you soon," Hawk said before adjusting his goggles over his eye. He jumped into the water and began his descent to the bottom.

Though Hawk had lights, he didn't need them at first. The water appeared surprisingly clear for the first twenty meters. But as he dove downward, a milky substance clouded his vision. Hawk activated the lights on his goggles and continued on.

However, Hawk never made it to the bottom before an object shot right past him.

What the hell was that?

He stopped and looked upward to see what appeared to be two men clutching sea scooters and moving straight toward him. Hawk noticed one of the men had a spear and quickly deduced that was the object that had just flown past.

Hawk reached for the knife he'd put in the holster around his shin and prepared for a fight.

About five meters away, the two men split up, forcing Hawk to choose where to go. He preferred to go after the spearman instead of getting tangled up with the other man before getting shot in the back.

The man zipped by and circled around.

Hawk turned off his lights and descended in an attempt to level the playing field. Without a sea scooter, he could only hope to strike a glancing blow as the men raced by.

Hawk wondered who the men were as he waited to strike. He watched for the lights of the men and tried to sense their direction from the hum of their propulsion devices. Scanning the water for bubbles wasn't the best option either since his field of vision was limited due to the darkness and murky water.

Just as Hawk was growing impatient, one of the men came zooming past. Struggling to turn his spear around, he appeared to be as taken aback as Hawk was.

Hawk seized his opportunity, reaching for the man's spear and yanking it out of his hands. However, the man didn't give up without a fight, engaging Hawk with hands.

The man pulled out a knife, matching Hawk weapon for weapon. Treading water, the two men jockeyed for position before the attacker struck first. Hawk rolled out of the way and jammed his knife into the man's arm. The man flailed at Hawk, missing him but slashing his air tube. Blood spewed from the man's arm, but Hawk caught him smiling. He motioned toward the sea floor and then pointed above before he shrugged, his pantomimed message clear to Hawk: The weapon or me—what is it going to be?

The other man swooped in to drag his partner to the surface, while the injured man waved mockingly at Hawk.

Hawk had no choice, though disabling the weapon seemed like the last thing he'd do before drowning in the Strait of Hormuz.

He reactivated his lights and held his breath. Once he reached the bottom, he located the launcher and progressed through the steps Dr. Morton had given him. The key was removing a communication chip that essentially served as the device's brain. Working quickly, Hawk opened a compartment that housed the chip and yanked it out. The device went dead, and Hawk began his ascent to the surface.

He went over all the possible scenarios as he rose to the top. He could be recaptured and dragged aboard or immediately killed in some other manner. Whatever the circumstance, he resolved not to go down without taking them out with him.

But Hawk wasn't prepared for what he saw when he reached the surface—the boat was gone. The only thing left was Abid's body floating in the water.

Hawk gasped for air as he removed the dead weight in the form of oxygen tanks from his back. He found his emergency flare gun and fired it, hoping someone would see it and pick him up.

Rolling over onto his back, Hawk broke into the backstroke. He figured he wouldn't make it to land, but the closer he was, the better chance he'd have at someone finding him.

But it didn't take long for someone to notice his flare. Ten minutes after he fired it, a fishing boat puttered up next to him. Once the fishermen noticed Hawk, they tossed a line to him and helped him aboard.

Hawk explained that someone had attempted to

murder him while exploring the water and left him to die. He asked the men to take him back to Kumzar, and they obliged.

As they cruised back, Hawk couldn't stop thinking about Alex. She was a sitting target, unaware that anyone was on to her—and Hawk had no way to notify her. He watched in the distance as the Kumzari harbor came into view.

Hawk was still looking when an explosion rocked the mainland. He glanced up in horror to see a portion of the Shati Albahr Inn blown apart and a fire raging. With his mouth agape, Hawk stared at the unfolding scene while the fishermen chattered among themselves.

That was our room.

CHAPTER 26

HAWK EXPRESSED HIS GRATITUDE to the fishermen and focused on the harbor ahead. The moment their ship came within leaping distance of the dock, he jumped and hit the wooden boards with a hard thud but maintained his balance. Breaking into a sprint, he rushed toward the hotel.

Chaos filled the streets as a crowd rushed toward the explosion. However, about halfway up the hill, people streamed downward, running away from the fiery inn. Sensing a difficult navigation ahead, Hawk darted to the outside to circumvent the crowds.

"Alex! Alex!" he called, scanning the mass of humanity for her face.

Nothing.

Hawk raced farther up the hill, his legs burning as they churned. Moving so swiftly, he barely felt his feet touch the ground.

Once he reached the top, several law enforcement

officials put up a hand to Hawk, warning him to stay back.

"It's not safe," an elderly said in Arabic. "Don't try to go in there, please. I beg you."

Hawk sighed and ignored the man, breaking past the negligible barrier of men and running toward the burning site. Dark smoke billowed upward. The surrounding area was filled with an eerie silence, broken only by crumbling rubble and the blaring fire alarm.

Navigating the debris, Hawk pressed on until he reached the back of the hotel. There wasn't a soul to be found.

Hawk returned to the perimeter the officials had set up.

"I was staying here," Hawk said to the man who'd tried to stop him earlier. "Why aren't you trying to save everyone? There must be people inside who are injured."

"The fire alarm went off five minutes before the explosion," the man said. "There was smoke coming from the elevator. No one was inside when the hotel exploded, at least not that we know of. Allah has had mercy on us all."

Hawk turned and ran back down the hill.

It wasn't Allah, old man. It was Alex.

Hawk didn't stop running until he reached the airfield. He ran up to the sole hangar and saw a man rubbing his hands with a greasy rag.

"Are you Mr. Hawk?" the man asked.

Hawk nodded.

"Good," the man said. "We've been expecting you."

"We?" Hawk asked.

Alex emerged from a door behind the man and greeted Hawk with a big grin.

"I thought you were dead," he said. "When I saw that big explosion while still out at sea, I figured they'd caught you for sure. But . . ."

"But then you found out someone pulled the fire alarm first?"

"That's when I knew it was you," Hawk said. "Those thugs would've just let everyone else die as well. Only you would've been so thoughtful before blowing up the place."

She laughed. "A woman's gotta do what a woman's gotta do. I knew you were in trouble and Al Hasib's men were on to us. Had to leave no doubt that I was dead. I faked my own death and slipped down here wearing a burqa. Spying as a woman in Muslim countries has its advantages."

"And how'd you make a bomb like that on the fly?"

"Gas stove, toaster fire—it wasn't rocket science. You need to tell me what happened to you. I was listening in up until the point that two men boarded *The Marlin* before tossing your earpiece overboard."

"I'll fill you in on our way," Hawk said. "Now, let's get out of here. We've neutralized the threat, and I'm ready to get home for some much-needed time off."

Alex dug into her backpack and pulled out a phone. "Do you want me to do the honors or are you saving that for yourself?"

"What are you talking about?"

"We need to tell Blunt it's over."

Hawk shook his head. "Let's just wait and tell him later. I'm exhausted right now, and the last thing I want to do is explain to him all the loose ends we've left here."

"I think we've left everything nice and tidy," she said.

"Aside from that big hole in the Shati Albahr Inn."

"We're both intact, and nobody knows it was us."

"Nor will they," Hawk said as he tossed their backpacks to the pilot so he could weigh them.

"Let's hope it stays that way."

Hawk turned to the pilot. "Are we good on weight?"

The pilot flashed a thumbs-up sign and motioned for them to get in the plane.

Hawk held the seat back for Alex before climbing in after her.

"Cozy," she said.

"And no place to stick your head out in case you get sick," Hawk said. "Are you sure you can handle this better?"

"Without a doubt."

CHAPTER 27

Washington, D.C.

BLUNT WIPED THE SLEEP out of his eyes as he
awoke to the television still on in the living room.
After falling asleep in the recliner, he never woke in
the middle of the night to get in his bed. And neither
did the FBI agent tasked with watching him. Blunt ad-
mired the man's dedication yet seized the moment and
took full advantage of his slumber. The agent clutched
the remote even as he slept but left his phone lying on
the end table. With the other agent already in bed,
Blunt snatched the cell that had taunted Blunt before
he fell asleep.

The floor creaked as Blunt eased down the hallway toward the bathroom. The guard stirred for a few
seconds but remained asleep. Turning the water on,
Blunt sat on the toilet and called Hawk on his burner
cell.

"I don't have long to talk," Blunt said as Hawk answered the phone.

"Where are you?" Hawk asked. "It sounds like you're on the river."

"It's a long story, but the short version is that I'm in FBI custody. How are things going with you?"

"Great," Hawk said. "Alex and I just completed the mission. We rendered the weapons system inoperable but had to leave it there due to unforeseen circumstances. I'll send you the coordinates for it later so you can send someone else to collect it. We're in Muscat now, but we're going to get some rest and relaxation somewhere in the Caribbean—at least that's the plan."

"You might want to put a hold on those plans. We've got bigger problems now."

"Bigger problems than Al Hasib wreaking havoc in the Strait of Hormuz?"

"Karif Fazil is here in the U.S., and he's plotting something in New York in the coming days."

"Wait. Back up. How did Fazil even get in the country?"

"I can't explain everything right now. But you two better get back here ASAP. Whatever Fazil is up to, I can promise you it won't be good. He's failed a couple of times before but only because of you."

Hawk sighed. "It's never easy, is it?"

Heavy footsteps storming down the hall startled Blunt. "Look, I gotta go, but I'll track you down once you get back."

Blunt flushed the toilet as the agent pounded on the door.

"I'll be out in just a minute," Blunt said.

"Where's my phone?" the agent roared.

Blunt deleted the number he'd just called and feigned ignorance.

"How should I know?" Blunt said, slipping it into his pocket. "You guys wouldn't let me call my own mother if she was on her deathbed."

The agent stomped back down the hall, and Blunt exhaled. He had to figure out a way to get the Firestorm team involved in stopping Fazil—and fast.

* * *

HAWK RELAYED THE conversation with Blunt to Alex as they waited for their plane to arrive at the gate at the Muscat International Airport.

"You need to put an end to this," Alex said. "Karif Fazil and his Al Hasib thugs are going to continue inflicting their terror on us if you don't do something to stop it."

Hawk forced a smile. "*We* need to put an end to this. Remember, we're a team. We do things together. Just because I'm the one on the forefront doing things doesn't mean I'm working solo here."

"You're right," Alex said. "I'm just frustrated—and I need a vacation."

"Perhaps we can do something about that soon enough. In the meantime, we can't really worry about this until we get back to Washington and get briefed on what's going on."

"Sounds like Blunt doesn't know much himself," Alex said. "Didn't you say it sounded like he was in a river? What's he doing in FBI custody?"

"Who knows? I haven't looked at the news in quite a while, but I'm sure we can find something about it on the internet. In the meantime, we need to think about what Fazil might do."

Alex crossed her arms. "Clearly, this whole stunt was a diversion. Fazil wanted us to come after this so he could have time to do whatever it is he's doing back home."

"Whatever Fazil is up to, Blunt sounded scared."

"Scared? Blunt?"

"Yeah, I know. It's unusual, but I heard a tremor in his voice."

"So, now what?"

Hawk's eyes widened. "First things first. I need to call Thomas Colton and let him know that we neutralized his weapon."

"I'm sure he'll sleep better at night."

"I doubt he's lost a wink of sleep over the whole ordeal."

Hawk pulled out his phone and dialed Colton's number.

"I've got some good news for you," Hawk said.

"Brady! It's so good to hear your voice," Colton replied.

"If you think the sound of my voice is good, wait until you hear what I'm about to say—we disarmed the weapon."

"That's wonderful."

Hawk caught a tinge of reticence in Colton's tone.

"Is everything all right?" Hawk asked.

"Well, first off, I'm glad you disabled the weapon. I appreciate what you did to make sure there wasn't a crisis in the Strait of Hormuz. I hope it wasn't too difficult for you."

Hawk huffed a soft laugh through his nose. "I guess that assessment would be relative."

"Secondly, there's something you need to know."

"I'm listening."

Colton sighed. "I just found this out myself and haven't found the gumption to call J.D. and let him know about it. But I need to let someone know as soon as possible because it's important."

"What happened?"

"Al Hasib stole something far more dangerous than our prototype torpedo weapons system, but nobody noticed it until now."

"What did they take?"

"We developed a suitcase nuke."

Hawk laughed nervously. "Seriously?"

"Yeah. It's heavy as hell, but it will actually fit in a briefcase."

"And what kind of damage can a weapon like that do?"

"It could wipe out a square mile in a city, maybe more."

"That's all?" Hawk asked.

"I wish I had better news, but we just found out about it. Al Hasib's theft was actually all about that. The weapons system was just to throw us off track."

"They did a damn good job, didn't they?"

"I wish you weren't right, but you are. They fooled us all."

Hawk sighed. "That'll be like looking for a needle in a haystack."

"Except you don't even know where the haystack is."

"Actually, I do. It's New York City, which doesn't help much. But I'll be in touch," Hawk said before he hung up.

He looked at Alex, his face telling.

"What is it?" she asked.

"Al Hasib stole a true suitcase nuke," Hawk said. "We're screwed."

He picked up his phone and started dialing another number.

"Who are you calling now?" she asked.

"I'm calling the president."

* * *

NOAH YOUNG LOOKED at the number on his phone and closed his eyes. He didn't want to take Brady Hawk's call. If anyone learned that they were communicating, Young's political future could be in jeopardy. With all the alleged links between Young and Blunt, adding a former Navy Seal to a list of connections could be all that Peterson needed to seize control of the election narrative a few weeks before the vote. The news report suggesting that maybe Conrad Michaels didn't actually die of natural causes—and that at least one black ops agent was at Camp David—was already becoming a growing headache for Young. And if someone tied Young to Hawk in the public sphere, Young's campaign could be sunk.

"People before politics," Young said to himself as he begrudgingly answered the phone.

"Talk to me," Young said.

"Mr. President, I wanted to call you with a report. I gather that Blunt's hands might be tied at the moment, and I need to speak with you about a potential terrorist threat in New York City."

"I had my security briefing this morning and am

well aware of all the threats against us."

"Including what's happening with Al Hasib?"

Young scowled and sifted through some papers on his desk. "I don't recall seeing anything like that."

"If that's the case, there's something going on that the FBI doesn't want you to know about for some reason," Hawk said. "But it's a grave threat, and it requires your immediate attention."

"I appreciate your concern, Brady, but I'm in the middle of a campaign here. I've got enough troubles of my own. I'm sure the FBI can handle any threats without my help. They're a capable organization."

"I understand, sir. But this isn't just another baseless threat—and the FBI knows it."

"Then let them handle it. I have more pressing matters at the moment."

"Sir, I wouldn't insist, much less call you and waste your precious time, unless this were of the utmost importance."

"I've already told you—"

"Mr. President, Karif Fazil is in New York City and has a stolen prototype suitcase nuke developed by Colton Industries. Now, I know you're focused on the campaign, but if this thing detonates in the next couple of days, thousands of people could die. And it'll happen on your watch. Any hope you might have of winning the election will be gone with Fazil's strike."

"This doesn't seem possible. How come nobody ever told me about this threat?"

"I can't answer that, sir, but I know Fazil better than anybody. I can help put a stop to this."

"Report to the FBI offices in New York and offer your services. I need to talk to my Homeland Security secretary about what's going on and will make sure you're working with the point people on this."

"Thank you, sir," Hawk said. "I know you've wanted to eliminate Al Hasib for this very reason. Getting Fazil will be a good start."

"Make it happen and good luck."

"You, too, Mr. President."

Young threw his head back and stared at the ceiling. He could sense his dream of winning the presidency slipping away—and even as the most powerful man in the free world, he felt powerless to stop it.

CHAPTER 28

New York City

HAWK AND ALEX TOOK A TAXI straight to the
FBI offices in New York once their plane landed. A
team of five federal agents greeted them in the lobby
and supplied them with the proper credentials. A lanky
bespectacled fellow named Richard Paxton introduced
himself as the lead FBI director on the case.

"You come highly recommended," Paxton said
as he shook Hawk's and Alex's hands. "As in, you can't
really get a much higher recommendation than that of
the president."

Paxton proceeded to introduce the rest of the
team, including Justin Frazier from NSA.

"Now that we're all acquainted, let's go upstairs
and get to work," Paxton said, ushering everyone into
the elevator. "From what I understand, we don't have
much time."

"The first question I have is do we have any leads?" Hawk asked.

The group was silent, all turning to Paxton. He pushed his glasses up on his nose and looked at his feet.

"We're still working on that," Paxton admitted. "We've heard some chatter from some sleeper cells that we recently reactivated, but nothing actionable yet. It's most unfortunate for us that the people we had embedded in several cells across the country with ties to Al Hasib are not privy to any potential plot."

Paxton pressed the button for the fifteenth floor, and the doors closed.

The ride up was awkwardly silent. Hawk wasn't sure if they were expecting him to come up with a potential target on the spot, but he was stunned that nobody at the agency had narrowed down the possibilities.

"How long has this team been working together?" Hawk asked in an attempt to defuse the tension.

"Less than a week," Paxton said. "You'll find it's a dedicated crew. If anybody can sniff out where Al Hasib intends to strike, I'm sure they can."

"Hmm," Hawk said, choosing to say nothing else. He noted that the NSA had a presence on the team. And while such a decision might be an effort to demonstrate interagency unity, Hawk saw it as nothing but a looming problem, if it hadn't already become one. The turf wars often existed because of each director's desire to receive full credit for the victory, sacrificing long-term results for short-term wins. Ultimately, the quest to climb any government agency's ladder exceeded any attempts at vanquishing an enemy. Many times a partial victory was deemed satisfactory and racked up enough good will to earn a promotion. The whole system made Hawk sick.

The elevator crawled to a halt, and the doors slid open. Hawk stepped off and waited for Paxton to lead them the war room. Pushing his way through the team, he emerged and gestured for everyone to follow. Several agents approached Paxton with documents for his signature, which he provided with hardly a glance.

Paxton took a seat at the head of the long table and invited the rest of the team to sit. Several monitors hung from the walls, and a large touch screen monitor was directly behind Paxton. He gestured for one of his assistants to hand out a report he had prepared about Karif Fazil.

Hawk opened to the first page and read the bio about Fazil. Simplistic in nature and lacking any details necessary to capture the Al Hasib leader, Hawk slammed the document shut.

"Is there something wrong, Mr. Hawk?" Paxton asked.

Hawk was about to speak when he watched Thomas Colton slip into the room and take a seat at the table.

"Don't stop on my account," Colton said as he made eye contact with Hawk.

Hawk took a deep breath and exhaled. "I know all about Karif Fazil, and the key to finding him won't be buried in a report like this."

"Please, by all means, enlighten us," Paxton said.

Hawk stood and paced around the room as he spoke. "Karif Fazil is not someone to be dissected through FBI psychological evaluations. He's a simple man on a simple mission—revenge. A U.S. mission several years ago killed his brother. That should tell you what you need to know about Fazil. He wants to inflict the most pain possible on our country. This isn't some idealistic jihadist. He wants blood, and nothing else will satisfy him. That's why we must catch him before he unleashes his fury on this city. Because I can assure you that whatever he's planning, it has the potential to kill thousands of people."

Alex nodded at Hawk.

"Alex knows Fazil, too," he said. "Is there something you see?"

"Based on all the potential targets, there's one that jumps out at me this week," she said.

"We've been over this list many times," Paxton

said. "Nothing seems like a slam dunk based on the numbers."

"This isn't about the sheer size of a crowd, though that could come into play," Alex said. "When I look at this list, I have to go all the way to the bottom to find his likely target—the Veteran's Day Parade."

Paxton laughed, shaking his head. "Ms. Duncan, what makes you think he'd target such a poorly-attended event like that one? Why not the Jets game on Sunday or the concert Saturday at Madison Square Garden?"

"With all due respect, sir," Alex began, "I don't think you're listening to what I'm saying. Karif Fazil wants to make a statement. A Taylor Swift concert wouldn't make a statement. A Jets game wouldn't make a statement. And—"

"How could you even say that with a straight face?" Paxton interrupted. "Taylor Swift is an American icon, and blowing up an arena where she is singing would create such visibility for the event that Al Hasib would be on the lips of every person around the globe twenty-four hours later."

"She has marginal talent with a keen eye for marketing," Alex said, wagging her finger. "Let's not act as if she's the second coming of Michael Jackson."

"If Swift's concert isn't the target, striking at the heart of American culture during an NFL game would also yield prime results for Fazil," Paxton said.

"Please, Mr. Paxton. The Jets and the Bills? Nobody is watching that dumpster fire of a game."

"So instead Al Hasib will concentrate their efforts on sabotaging a parade that likely ninety-nine percent of Americans don't even know exists—and that's being generous."

"I'll bet ninety-nine New Yorkers don't even know about it," Justin Frazier chimed in.

"But it might be more popular this year," Alex said. "It says in your report that the grand marshal is presidential candidate James Peterson."

"And that's exactly why we can't shut it down, even if we wanted to," Paxton said.

"Does Peterson know about the threat?" Alex asked. "I'm sure he wouldn't mind hearing about it from someone."

Hawk watched as Frazier and Paxton communicated with glances at each other, though neither saying a word.

"Why do I get the feeling there's something else going on you're not telling me?" Hawk asked.

Paxton crossed his arms and leaned back in his chair. "There are some things we're just not at liberty to discuss with you."

"If we're going to catch Fazil before he strikes, you need to tell me everything," Hawk said.

"Can't do it," Paxton said. "It'd jeopardize the entire operation."

"So this is just part of an *operation*?" Hawk asked as he shook his head in disbelief. "What are you guys doing? I imagine this means you *knew* Fazil was coming here but you let him in anyway. Who are you trying to catch here? A terrorist or someone else?"

"Look, Mr. Hawk, I appreciate your vigilance in wanting to apprehend Karif Fazil before he kills hundreds—"

"Thousands," Hawk corrected.

"Okay, thousands of innocent Americans. But our past decisions about why we did what we did is of little relevance at this point to you."

"It's actually very relevant," Hawk said as he narrowed his eyes. "If you want this blood-thirsty terrorist caught, you can't leave me in the dark about anything. Need I remind you that innocent lives are at stake? And you need my help to avoid another tragedy."

"I promise to share all the pertinent information with you, Mr. Hawk," Paxton said. "And I promise that you'll understand our reasons later, but for now, you're going to have to trust me."

"Then I suggest you trust me, too, and cancel the Veteran's Day parade," Hawk said.

"We can't," Frazier said, leaning forward as he interjected. "Peterson won't have it. He'll see this as some political revenge by Noah Young for accusing him of live streaming a meeting with a Russian ambassador."

"You're going to allow this event to take place even though it's a likely target for Fazil?" Hawk asked. His jaw fell agape after he finished.

"Right now, the bureau can't afford to wade into the waters of some political game. We need to maintain the public's trust that we're an objective government agency."

Hawk sat back down and stacked the document on the table in front of him. "If the public finds out that you didn't cancel the parade for political reasons, you're not going to have a shred of the public's trust moving forward."

"That's a chance we're willing to take, Mr. Hawk," Paxton said. "Now I think we need to stop debating something that's not to happen regarding the parade and focus on what we can do to stop this."

"What are you doing in the way of facial recognition?" Alex asked.

"Good question," Paxton said. "Let me get one of my agents in here who's overseeing that part of the operation."

As he got up, the door swung open, and a woman carrying a tablet entered the room.

"I apologize for interrupting, sir," she said, "but you need to see this."

"What is it?" Paxton asked as he reached for the tablet.

"Our facial recognition software is going berserk. We've had more than a hundred hits on Karif Fazil in the last hour. And unless he's got some superhuman speed and is racing back and forth across the city, there's a major problem."

"Why don't you put this on the monitors so everyone can see," Paxton said.

The woman complied, and the hits of Karif Fazil's face populated a map of the city along with the time that it occurred. His image was clustered around a handful of city blocks.

"Where is this?" Hawk asked.

Alex glanced at her notes. "It's all along the parade route for tomorrow."

"He's just messing with you—or making a practice run," Hawk said.

Paxton closed his eyes and sighed as he shook his head. "We're still not canceling the parade."

"Then we're going to have a big problem tomorrow at the parade—and an even bigger mess to clean up," Hawk said.

"Let's just keep working," Paxton said. "We're all smart enough to figure out a way to stop this madman."

"From what I've found, tracking terrorists across the Middle East, when someone is desperate and determined, your odds of success aren't good," Hawk said.

"But there's still a chance, right?" Paxton asked.

Hawk shrugged. "It's possible."

"Then find a way to catch this guy before he does something we'll all regret."

CHAPTER 29

New York City

JAMES PETERSON SLIPPED into the backseat of the convertible before looking up at the gray New York sky. The cloud cover combined with the looming buildings made for a dark day. Jamming his hands into his coat pockets, Peterson shivered and scanned the staging area for the Veterans Day parade.

"Is anybody even going to attend this thing today?" Peterson asked his campaign advisor, who had his head buried in his notes.

"Absolutely, sir. It's going to be packed. The campaign offices here have done a great job of getting the word out about the event. The footage will look fantastic on television later tonight."

Peterson glanced at his watch and cracked his knuckles. "What time are we going to get started? I thought we would be moving by now."

"Patience, sir. We have a few more minutes before we leave. And I believe we're also waiting on your son."

Peterson groaned and looked for William, his son who seemed to find trouble even when it didn't exist. Over the past few years, William had made an incredible turnaround regarding his drug and alcohol addiction. After a few months at one of the nation's top rehab centers, William emerged clean and sober for the first time since he was in high school. But Peterson knew his son's mischief wasn't limited to substance abuse.

"I hope Little Willie isn't up to no good," Peterson said.

William hopped into the convertible and landed on the back seat just to the right of his father. "I thought I told you that I hate the nickname *Little Willie.*"

"Start acting like a grownup, and I'll call you William," Peterson said. He checked his watch again. "Seriously, when is this thing going to start? I've got a rally to get to later this afternoon."

The car lurched forward as it started to roll.

"Looks like we're getting started now," Peterson's campaign manager said.

The convertible turned to the right and eased onto the parade route. Peterson squinted as he scanned the street ahead to see what kind of turnout would be there to greet him.

"Doesn't look like the crowd is all that big," Peterson said.

"Just wait, sir."

Peterson looked at William, who fidgeted with his fingers.

"Do you have a problem, Little Willie?" Peterson asked.

William stared off in the distance before responding. "Look, Dad, there's something I need to tell you."

"Oh, Lord," Peterson said. "Please tell me you haven't murdered anyone."

"No, no one's been murdered."

"Thank God. What is it, son? I can take anything now."

William looked at his hands and rubbed them before responding. "I might have done something that might not cast you in the best light."

Peterson eyed his son closely. "Go on."

"You know when you said that we need to make sure that the American people know that Noah Young doesn't care about homeland security?"

"Yes, I remember. That's an area I am hammering him in."

"Well, I might have made sure the American people recognize that for sure."

Peterson cocked his head to one side. "I'm not sure I'm following you, son."

"What I'm trying to say is that I kind of struck a deal with someone from Al Hasib, who plans to unleash a terrorist strike on U.S. soil in the coming weeks."

"You did *what*?"

"I know, I know. In hindsight, it wasn't the best idea."

"*Hindsight*? What about foresight? Son, if anyone finds out about this, it's a disaster."

"I realize that now."

"What were you thinking? And what did you do exactly?"

"Here it goes," William mumbled. "I used your plane to sneak Karif Fazil into the country."

"I should knock your lights out right now," Peterson said. "And if the camera weren't rolling, I'd do it. I'd kick your ass and leave you on the street. You're lucky you're telling this to me now."

"But it's worse than that," William said as he stared off in the distance.

"Worse than that? How is that even possible?" Peterson said, his mouth falling open.

"I've seen Karif Fazil at the parade site today. I think he's planning something."

"Are you serious? You invited that scumbag here, and now he's going to kill us?"

William cringed and hunched over, appearing to brace for a blow from his father.

"Stop with that," Peterson said. "I'm not going to hit you now. But I just might beat you senseless later on."

"It wouldn't be the first time."

"Watch your mouth, Son. You only have yourself to blame for such a ridiculous action." Peterson peered at the road ahead. "Driver, I think we're done here. Can you take the next road to the left and return us back to the staging area?"

"No can do," the driver said. "I'm being paid to drive a route. And if you're in my car, you're going with me."

"Like hell I am," Peterson said. "We're all going to die if we stay the course."

"I'm sorry there isn't a bigger crowd here, sir, but a job's a job," the driver said. "And my job is to drive you along the parade route."

"Well, I know this is above your security clearance, but there is an active terror threat along this parade route."

"According to who? I know you're just embarrassed, sir. And I can't really blame you. But until I hear otherwise from my superiors, I'm going to do what I was asked to do."

Peterson hunched down and spoke sternly in the ear of the man seated behind the steering wheel. "Turn this car around right now and get me back to the staging area or else I'm going to beat your ass right here."

The driver turned around and glared at Peterson. "I'd like to see you try."

Peterson stood in the back seat before raising his leg and kicking at the back of the driver's head. The driver grabbed for Peterson's leg and missed as the car began to weave back and forth across the road. Undaunted by his first failed attempt to stop the driver, Peterson made a second attempt, this time connecting with a solid kick. Dazed by the hit, the driver swayed back and forth before collapsing across the seat. His head rested in the passenger's seat.

Peterson yanked the driver's body over to the passenger seat and slipped down behind the wheel. He jerked it to the right and looped back toward the staging area.

In the back, William gasped several times. After the fifth time, Peterson said something. "What's wrong with you back there?"

William's voice trembled as he spoke. "Karif Fazil—he's, he's, he's everywhere."

"What do you mean *everywhere*?"

"I mean, I've seen him five times already."

"Is this Karif Fazil guy also an Olympic sprinter? I'm not going that slow, but not fast enough that he could circle the block five times since I took the wheel."

"No, it's just that—I've seen five men that look like him. He's up to something."

Peterson glanced over his shoulder and narrowed his eyes.

"I swear, if you weren't related to me, I just might drive this car over the Brooklyn Bridge and pray that you don't make it out alive."

"I'm sorry, Dad," William said. "I was just trying to help."

"Maybe the only way you can help is by staying out of the way."

"That's what I'll do then," William said. "I'll vanish. I'll disappear. You won't see me until after you've already been elected President."

"I think it's too late now," Peterson said. "The damage is done. I just hope we can survive the night."

Peterson jammed his foot onto the accelerator and gripped the steering wheel tightly. But it didn't matter. He could already feel the presidency slipping out of his grasp—all thanks to his treasonous son.

Peterson knew it wasn't right for a father to feel like he did, but he secretly hoped that William would get caught and spend the rest of his life in jail.

It'd be better than trying to make excuses for him for the rest of my life.

But Peterson couldn't dwell on that fact for long. As long as he was on the ballot, he still had a chance to win. That also meant he still had a candidate to destroy.

CHAPTER 30

KARIF FAZIL WORE A SMUG GRIN on his face as he strode through the streets of New York. The intersecting routes he created and assigned to each of his lookalikes produced the type of chaos he'd hoped for. Using another piece of technology he'd stolen from Katarina Petrov before her death, he had masks produced for each of the three hundred men who'd agreed to be part of the plot. And as they all strode through the city, no one could tell them apart.

Right before all the men dispersed from the warehouse, Fazil delivered a stirring speech. He encouraged all of them to carry out their duty with pride, warning them of the possibility of arrest if law enforcement uncovered their plot.

"But that won't stop us," Fazil said. "It won't stop our jihad!"

The men had roared with approval, their cheers still echoing in Fazil's ears as he walked. If he was honest with himself, he knew he could've guaranteed success by simply dropping off the bomb in the middle of a city park and detonating it. But Fazil wanted credit. He wanted the world to know Al Hasib was behind the attack. And he wanted U.S. officials to know that he'd only just begun to avenge his brother's death.

Fazil squeezed through a congested area as a crowd began to form along the street in preparation for the parade. He reveled in the fact that he could pull off this attack in broad daylight while surrounded by hundreds of police officers. With their eyes scanning the crowd constantly for any potential threats to the floats, bands, and people in the street, the cops didn't have time to inspect every suspicious person.

As Fazil rounded a corner, he felt a strong hand grab his shoulder.

"You're going to need to come with me," the man said.

Fazil stopped and turned around, coming face to face with a man holding up his FBI badge.

With wide eyes, Fazil stepped back. "What did I do? I'm just walking the streets, minding my own business. This is profiling."

The agent ignored Fazil's accusation. "I need to inspect the contents of your briefcase."

"How dare you," Fazil said indignantly. "I am a law-abiding citizen of this country. You can't just order me somewhere because you think I'm a criminal. I have rights—and I know them."

"Save it for the lawsuit," the agent said. "We still need to look through your briefcase."

"This is an outrage," Fazil said. "You better believe I'll be contacting my lawyer when this is all over with and suing you for every penny you've got."

The agent laughed and shook his head as he opened the briefcase. "And when you've spent every last dime on lawyers, maybe you'll get a free ticket out of here."

The briefcase fell open, and folders and papers spilled onto the ground. Kneeling to collect all the documents, the agent let out a string of expletives.

"What did you expect to find?" Fazil said, chiding the man. "Did you think I was carrying a weapon around in there? You're pathetic—and I'm going to sue you. What's your name?"

"Joe Friday," the agent replied.

"A federal agent and a funny one at that."

The agent shut the briefcase and shoved it into Fazil's chest. "Have a nice day."

Fazil smiled as the agent spun on his heels and walked away.

"Oh, I will," Fazil said. "Don't you worry."

He opened his jacket and peeked at the gas mask he'd partially stashed in an inner pocket.

"Just you wait."

CHAPTER 31

HAWK SIPPED A CUP OF COFFEE and watched the chaos swirling around the FBI offices as the Veteran's Day parade began in earnest. A bank of screens displayed various camera images from closed circuit televisions located along the route. With handfuls of folders, agents hustled back and forth across the room, rushing to examine the latest facial recognition photo of Karif Fazil.

Hawk turned to Alex. "Does this make you appreciate our small team or what?"

Alex laughed. "You'd think these people have never dealt with terrorists before."

"Maybe they haven't," Hawk said.

"Well, why don't you go show them how it's done, okay?"

Hawk approached Richard Paxton, who gulped a large cup of coffee from Starbucks and wore a permanent scowl across his forehead.

"Can I be of any assistance to you, sir?" Hawk asked.

"We sure could use your help in finding Fazil," Paxton said. "We've already received nearly 200 hits on facial recognition, though I'm not sure any of the men are him."

"This is just what he was doing yesterday in the trial run."

"Yes, and we still haven't figured out a way to adjust the algorithms to identify precisely which one is him."

"Pulling his face out of a sea of lookalikes won't be easy."

"Well, if there's anything you can do to help in that matter—*anything*—I'd be most grateful."

Hawk walked up to the bank of monitors and eyed each one carefully.

"If you're going to figure this out, you better work fast," said a woman who hammered on a keyboard, sending each matched image to a separate screen and posting what percentage the program believed each particular face captured on camera was a match for Fazil.

"How many have you gone through?" Hawk asked.

"Thoroughly, we've checked about fifty so far," she said. "We're marking each one that we've already seen to avoid turning this project into a wasted exercise."

"It's hardly something I would consider a *project*."

"Until Fazil actually does something on American soil, I consider him little more than a pest."

"Don't underestimate him," Hawk said. "He's sly."

"And you're the great Brady Hawk who's supposedly interacted personally with him on his turf?" she said in a mocking manner. "Obviously, you're still alive, so he can't be *that* elusive."

"I'm very fortunate to be standing here," Hawk said.

"Right now, all you're doing is standing here depleting my oxygen while you yammer on about past exploits."

Hawk eyed her closely. "Have you had any coffee yet this morning? Perhaps I could get you a cup."

"Just find the damn terrorist so Paxton will stop crawling all over us, okay?"

Hawk nodded and stepped back from the bank of screens, scanning them as cameras zoomed in on men wearing the same suit and carrying the same briefcase by all the Fazil clones. He noticed a dark flash of something across one of the images as the camera swept across the street.

Hawk rushed up to the screen and pointed at it. "This one right here," he said. "Can someone zoom out with this camera and tell me where this is?"

"It's the corner of 28th and Broadway," one of the agents said.

Hawk waited for the camera to pull back and show a broader view of the surrounding area. Once he could see the whole street, he looked in the upper part of the picture and waited.

"What exactly are you looking for?" the woman asked.

Hawk waved her off.

"Maybe I can help," she persisted.

"I think I know," Alex said as she stepped next to Hawk. "Are you thinking what I'm thinking?"

Hawk nodded. "Fazil brought his damn bird with him. He won't go anywhere without it."

After a few seconds, Hawk watched Jafar soar above the street. Hawk pointed to the picture.

"Find the man on that street," he said. "That's where Fazil is."

"There's nobody that matches his suit anywhere on either sidewalk," one of the agents said.

"Alex, keep an eye out on that street for me," Hawk said as he walked hurriedly toward the door before stopping and tossing an earpiece at her.

"What are you doing?" Alex asked, glancing down at the device she'd caught.

"I'm going to go down there and find him myself," he said. "Get in my ear, and keep me informed about what's going on."

CHAPTER 32

HAWK RACED OUT OF THE DOORS of the FBI offices and headed toward 28th Street. As he ran, he went through a number of scenarios in his mind about what Fazil's next move might be. Ruling out a suicide bomb, Hawk knew Fazil was intent on making a splash but—in his arrogance—wanted to receive full credit for Al Hasib. Hawk was determined to prevent any such twisted glory for Fazil.

Hawk touched his finger to his ear, re-securing the device.

"Alex, can you hear me?"

"Loud and clear," she said. "I'm following you on our cameras here. You're about a block away."

"Have you been able to find Fazil yet?"

"Not yet. I'm starting to think he's fooled us all."

"Well, if that bird is there, he is too. But perhaps he's not dressed like everyone else."

"I'll bet he's wearing a different mask, too."

"Bastard," Hawk said. "Don't worry. I'll be able to spot him once I get there."

"I just hope it's not too late," Alex said, her voice starting to tremble. "You better come back, Hawk."

"You're scared aren't you?"

"And you're not?"

"I'm always a little frightened when I'm running into something like this," Hawk said. "But I can't dwell on it. I've got a job to do—and I damn well better succeed. I don't have time to think about the consequences, and you shouldn't either. Let's stay focused. We'll get through this. This isn't any different than every other mission we've gone on."

She exhaled slowly. "Okay, I'll take your word for it. Just something about this seems bigger."

"It's New York," he said. "Everything here seems more dramatic."

She laughed softly. "How can you be so calm?"

"This is what I do, Alex. And I'm going to come back. I promise."

Hawk rounded the corner and looked up. After scanning the skyline, he spotted the bird circling overhead. Hawk looked directly beneath the bird and searched for Fazil.

"Come out, come out, wherever you are," Hawk said.

He spotted a man leaning up against the wall of

a building adjacent to a razed lot. A few feet away from him were the steps leading down into the 28th Street subway station.

That's gotta be Fazil.

Approaching the man cautiously, Hawk froze when the man looked up. He stared right at Hawk.

"Fancy seeing you here, Mr. Hawk," the man said.

Hawk reached for his gun and trained it on Karif Fazil.

"I bet you didn't think we'd meet like this again, did you?"

"Your eye has healed quite nicely," Fazil said as Jafar landed on his shoulder. "Too bad you're going to die today."

Hawk shook his head. "I think you've got it all wrong, that is unless you're prepared to die right now, too."

"Oh, I am," Fazil said, nodding. "I'm ready to make the ultimate sacrifice, if necessary. I'm just wondering if you're prepared to sacrifice all these innocent people here as well."

"You actually found the courage to blow yourself up for your cause instead of sending your men to do the dirty work for you?" Hawk said. "That's some bold leadership."

Fazil bit his lip and swung his briefcase in front of him, clutching it with both hands.

"Do you know what's inside here, Mr. Hawk?"

"I've heard you stole a suitcase nuke from Colton Industries, so I'm going to assume that's what you're carrying."

Fazil held up his briefcase and studied it for a moment. "I think this is more or less a *briefcase* nuke, but, nevertheless, I see you've done your homework."

"When I put a couple bullets in your chest, it won't matter because it's not going to detonate here."

Fazil cocked his head to one side. "I wouldn't be so sure of that. Let me ask you a question. Have you ever heard of a dead man's switch?"

"You want me to believe that you have one attached to that bomb?"

Fazil shrugged. "I'm not trying to get you to believe anything. I know the truth, and it's up to you whether or not you believe it, much like all the ridiculous things you Americans believe. But the point is, I do have one, and this bomb will go off if you shoot me."

Fazil held up a small cylindrical device, his thumb pressed firmly on top of it.

"Now, this detonator operates off a cell signal, and I've already activated it," Fazil continued. "All I have to do is let go and this bomb will explode, exposing everyone in about a mile radius or so to a deadly radiation. Many thousands of people will die.

And if you shoot me, I'll be among them. But you'll be executing yourself along with all the innocent Americans in this area. Let me go and maybe you'll figure out a way to defuse it. However, that will be the least of your worries."

Fazil raised his other hand in the air and signaled by twirling his index finger around several times. He set down his briefcase on the ground and stepped to the side. Seconds later, a legion of Fazil clones started dropping their briefcases on top of his.

Hawk watched in horror as the men filed by and disappeared down the steps into the 28th Street station.

As the scene unfolded in front of him, Hawk mulled over his options. Fazil may have been bluffing, but Hawk wasn't interested in the possibility of being wrong. Too much was at stake.

"What's going on down there?" Alex asked. "The FBI is ready to send in a dozen agents."

Hawk put his finger to his ear. "Tell them to back off. Fazil has a dead man's switch, and if he goes down the steps into the subway, we don't need him mobbed by any FBI personnel or else it's going to be sure death for everyone in the vicinity."

Hawk glanced over his shoulder at the parade as it rolled listlessly by. Veterans perched on floats waved to the crowd, all blissfully unaware of the impending danger unfolding just a few meters away.

When the last man dropped his briefcase on the pile, it had grown to about waist high and sprawled across the corner.

Fazil nodded at Hawk. "You've chosen wisely, Mr. Hawk. I commend you for your optimism, but I can assure you that you won't have time to escape. And follow me into the subway and I won't hesitate to release the bomb."

Fazil produced a gas mask from his pocket. "You don't have one of these on you, do you?"

Hawk watched helplessly as Fazil whispered something to Jafar. The bird took flight and soared above the street. Fazil waved at his bird before turning his attention back to Hawk.

"Good luck," Fazil called before he turned and vanished into the darkness.

Hawk didn't waste any time before springing into action.

"Where are those agents?" Hawk said. "I need them now."

"What do you need them to do?" Alex asked.

"I need them to help me find Fazil's suitcase and disarm the nuke before he detonates it."

"We don't have that kind of time," she said. "I heard what he said. Once he gets a safe enough distance away, he's going to come out of the subway and release the switch."

"Well, find me some time."

"I'm not a miracle worker, you know."

"How far do you think he'll have to go to be safe?"

"Everyone here at the bureau office thinks he'd head south and would likely get off at Washington Square. It'd be easy for him to disappear."

"Well, I'm counting on you to think of something."

Hawk motioned for the other agents to come over toward him and sort through the suitcases.

"Colton said the bomb weighed about fifty pounds, so it shouldn't take us more than a second or two to determine the weight," Hawk explained. "Let's toss them over to the side and form a discarded pile. If you happen to find the right one, let me know immediately."

Hawk and a half dozen agents sifted through the cases one by one. He had checked about twenty before he glanced at his watch.

"Alex, I had an idea," he said. "Why don't you hack the cell towers? Shut them down briefly. That could interrupt the signal."

"That'll take too long," she said. "Besides, I thought of something better—and more efficient."

"What's that?"

"I'm going to strand him in the subway."

"Are you sure which train he's on? He had a gas mask. It could all be part of another one of his bait-and-switch moves."

"It won't matter," she said. "I'm going to shut it all down."

"*You're* going to do this?" Hawk said as he picked up more suitcases, shaking them to determine the weight. "Why don't you have New York Metro shut their trains down for you?"

"Not enough time—and too much bureaucratic red tape. It's easier to do it this way and ask for forgiveness later."

"I doubt you'll have to ask for forgiveness if this works."

"It better work," she said. "You promised you were coming back."

"Yes, I did," Hawk said.

One of the agents yelped. "I found it."

Hawk rushed over to the man and took the suitcase from him. In a few seconds, Hawk managed to jimmy open the lock and stare at the elaborate design. "You've gotta be kidding me."

"What is it?" Alex asked.

"Give Colton your earpiece. I need him to tell me how to diffuse this thing."

"Okay, but work fast," Alex said.

"Have you got the trains stopped yet?"

"Not yet—still working on it."

Hawk stared at the intersecting wires and the flashing lights staring back at him.

"How far before his train reaches Washington Square?" he asked.

"One minute if I don't get it shut down. Here's Colton."

Hawk studied the bomb. "Tell me what I'm looking at here."

"It's complicated," Colton said. "So listen carefully."

* * *

FAZIL LOOKED AT HIS WATCH. The automated voice alerted the passengers to the name of the upcoming station.

"Next stop: Washington Square."

One more minute until Al Hasib becomes a name on the lips of everyone in the world. One more minute until the Americans regret killing my brother.

A satisfied smile swept across Fazil's face, but the grin vanished when the train jerked to a stop in the middle of the tunnel.

"Just great," mumbled a man. "More construction delays in the tunnels."

"Probably because of that damn parade," griped another woman.

"It's getting to the point that it's faster to walk," a man standing behind Fazil chimed in.

Fazil pulled his phone out of his pocket and noticed he didn't have a signal, which was typical for being stuck underground. He turned to the man behind him. "How far away from the platform are we?"

"Maybe another thirty seconds or so on the train."

"What about on foot?"

The man's eyes widened, and he leaned back from Fazil, studying him up and down.

"Do you have a death wish? You'd be a fool to try and run through the tunnels."

Fazil glanced at several of his men who'd boarded the train with him.

"What are you guys?" the stranger asked. "Part of some flash mob? Man, I hate those things."

"Rest easy, my friend. We're part of no such thing."

Fazil pushed his way past the man and through the crowded train car until he reached the back door. He forced it apart, squeezed through the opening, and broke into a sprint.

* * *

HAWK SNIPPED ONE OF THE WIRES and breathed a sigh of relief when nothing happened.

"You're doing great, Hawk," Colton said. "Just relax."

"What's next?" Hawk asked. "And how much time do I have?"

"You're going to sever the blue wire next."

Hawk's hand remained steady as he pinched the designated line and cut it with the scissors from his pocketknife.

"Alex wants you to know that she's got the subway system stopped, but Fazil's train was only one block from the platform."

"In other words, if he got off the train, I won't have much time."

"That's the assumption around here," he said. "The FBI has dispatched a dozen agents to Washington Square, but there's no guarantee how much time we have left."

Hawk wiped his brow with the back of his hand. "Just keep telling me what to do."

* * *

FAZIL SKIDDED TO A STOP when he saw several flashlights combing the darkness in front of him.

He climbed between a couple cars near the front and made his way to the opposite wall. Easing along toward the platform, he ducked into a maintenance hatch and waited for the flashlights to pass. He peered through the glass portal in the door and watched until the agents were hidden on the other side of the train.

Creeping back out into the tunnel, he gently shut the door and walked several meters before breaking into a sprint again.

"Look! Over there!" one of the agents shouted.

But Fazil knew it was too late. He had a huge head start and only needed to make it to the top before they did.

Without warning, the lights in the tunnel powered back on and the train began rumbling down the tracks behind him.

Fazil pumped his arms, knowing this was his moment for glory.

"*Allahu Akbar*!" he said to himself as he ran.

By the time he reached the station, the train was less than a hundred meters behind him.

Fazil scrambled up onto the platform and raced toward the stairs, jumping over the turnstiles and through the confused crowd of passengers awaiting the next train's arrival.

Hustling up the steps, he reached the top and realized his cell signal was at full strength. He quickly redialed the number with his right hand, while his left thumb was depressed on the detonator linked to the phone. After ringing once, a connection was made and a green light flashed on the device in his left hand.

"This is for you, brother," Fazil said.

He pulled his hand off the device and waited to hear an earth-rattling explosion north of his location.

But nothing happened.

"Come on," Fazil said as he pushed the button again and again.

Still nothing.

* * *

HAWK COLLAPSED next to the suitcase once he severed the final wire.

"It's finished," he announced.

Colton relayed the message, and Hawk listened as a raucous celebration occurred in the background.

"I knew you would do it," Alex said.

"You wrestled that earpiece away from Colton fast," Hawk said.

"He doesn't need it now. I think he's going to celebrate with a few drinks and try to forget this ever happened."

"Well, New York City would've been a mess without you, too. I knew you would think of something creative to buy me some time."

"That's all you needed, wasn't it?" she said. "Just a little bit more time?"

"I need to start realizing that any time I have is precious."

"Yeah, you're not invincible, though it sure does feel that way sometimes—just not when you're forced to disarm a nuclear weapon in the middle of Manhattan during a Veteran's Day parade."

Hawk stood and looked toward the street. Another float rolled by, packed with more oblivious veterans.

272 | R.J. PATTERSON

"This would've been a disaster."

"Let's not worry about what could've been," she said. "I say we join Colton and let him buy us some drinks."

Hawk grunted. "We're not done yet."

"What are you talking about?"

"Fazil. Where is he? We can't let him get out of the country, much less the city."

"Hang on," she said. "I know he was spotted at Washington Square Park a few minutes ago. Let me see what I can find out."

Hawk paced around the pile of suitcases and shook hands with the agents there, thanking them for their assistance. He realized just how vital each person's contribution was or else he would've been vaporized.

"Just got a report," Alex said. "And I'm afraid you're not going to like it."

"What is it?"

"Fazil is gone."

"What do you mean *gone*?"

"They can't find him anywhere. He vanished in the park."

"What about his bird?" Hawk said. "Look for Fazil's bird."

"They already did. It isn't there either. Fazil is gone."

CHAPTER 33

Washington, D.C.

HAWK AND ALEX MET WITH the joint task force of FBI and NSA officials at the Pentagon one week after the near tragedy in New York. He was surprised to see Blunt present at the meeting, especially given that Blunt had been essentially held captive during the sting operation to capture William Peterson.

"What's to become of Peterson's son?" Hawk asked as they sat down.

"We want to try him for treason," Justin Frazier said.

"But . . ." Hawk said, realizing Frazier wasn't done.

"It's political," Frazier said. "I prefer we treat him as a traitor and get it over with quickly."

"Well, he did invite a known terrorist into the country for the express purpose of killing innocent Americans," Blunt said.

"And I'm assuming Peterson claims he knew nothing of the plot," Hawk said.

"You'd be correct," Frazier said. "The FBI would have a difficult time winning that case, but the American voters are going to act as judge and jury in this instance. If the polls are any indication about what people think, a guilty verdict will be delivered by the American people in a few days and he'll slink back into obscurity in the political realm."

"As it should be," Blunt said. "How anyone could do such a thing is beyond me."

"So, why are we here?" Hawk said.

Frazier stood. "We know that the Firestorm team is one of the better kept secrets over the past few years in Michaels's administration."

"I hope you intend to keep it that way," Hawk said.

Frazier nodded. "Of course, but we also want to offer our assistance whenever possible."

"You mean like not trying to hunt me down when I re-task satellites for missions vital to our nation's security?" Alex asked.

"Exactly," said the FBI's Richard Paxton. "And I've been told to pass along apologies to you for that."

Alex shrugged. "I don't blame you really. It's not like I was exactly acting within the confines of the law."

"Yes, but in the future, we want to give you clearance, not make you hack our system and redirect satellites," Frazier said. "We need to expand the Firestorm team."

"I see what you're getting at, and my team isn't answering to anybody else," Blunt said.

"Now, J.D., wait just a—" Frazier said.

"No, Justin, we've been friends for a long time, long enough for me to know what's going on here," Blunt said. "If you want to give Alex access to your systems so she doesn't disrupt everything when she hacks into it, fine. But we're not going to notify anyone about what we're doing. I've found that in the world of espionage and subsequent assassinations, a small closed loop is the best loop of all."

"Don't be so closed-minded," Paxton said. "See how well we all worked together."

"It worked this time," Blunt said, "but it was a risky proposition. For God's sake, you guys arrested me and made me look like a fool to the nation."

"It worked, didn't it?" Frazier said.

"Yeah—and the apology and exoneration you issued will likely only be seen by about half of the people who read or heard about my original arrest."

"Settle down, J.D.," Paxton said. "This isn't about you."

"No, it's about my country and the fact that we

have to even have an outfit operate like this because there are always messes to clean up."

A woman knocked on the door and interrupted the meeting, whispering something in Frazier's ear.

"Excuse me," he said. "Apparently, someone needs to speak with our good friend Brady Hawk right now, and it's a conversation that can't wait."

Hawk stood and strode toward the door. "Who wants to talk with me?"

"It's the president, sir," the woman said as she led Hawk down the hallway to an unoccupied office where he could take the call.

Hawk settled into the chair and picked up the phone.

"Mr. President," Hawk began. "So nice of you to call."

Noah Young moaned. "So nice of you to save New York City last week. If you didn't need to remain so anonymous, I'd commemorate what you did by putting your face on some U.S. currency."

"Those are kind words, sir."

"And I mean them," Young said. "You saved my bacon, too."

"How did I do that?"

"It's a long story, but Peterson would've had me for lunch if the truth about what was going on with his live streaming event with the Russian ambassador ever leaked to the press."

"I guess we should be grateful that it didn't," Hawk said.

"Very grateful indeed."

"So, what's next, other than a rapidly approaching election?"

Young chuckled. "I'd love to wait until I take office to dispatch you to the Middle East again, but I'm afraid we don't have time. Fazil's latest brazen attempt to attack us on our own soil has me concerned. We narrowly avoided an unmitigated disaster, and this isn't the first time we've been able to do that. You've done a great job serving your country in this way, but I'm afraid you won't be able to succeed every time."

"So, what are you getting at, sir?"

"I want you to take the fight to him," Young said. "Go beat him on his home turf. Do whatever it takes to make sure he goes away for good."

"I'd love to do that for you, sir. But I do have one request."

"Name it."

"We need more resources. Gadgets, money, any technology to help us get an advantage for catching Fazil and putting an end to Al Hasib."

"Done," Young said. "You send me a list, and I'll make sure everything you need is put at the fingertips of you and Alex."

"And when do you want us to start?" Hawk asked.

278 | R.J. PATTERSON

"I've got a plane fueled up and waiting for you whenever you're ready to leave."

Hawk pumped his fist. "That's the best news I've heard all day."

He hung up and walked back into the meeting room.

"I hate to cut this meeting short, but the senator and Alex need to come with me immediately," Hawk said.

"Is there a problem?" Paxton asked.

"Yeah, and it won't get solved with us sitting around this table," Hawk said. "It's time for some serious action."

"What are you planning on doing?" Frazier asked.

Hawk grinned. "Hitting Al Hasib where it hurts the most and never letting it get up off the mat."

THE END

ACKNOWLEDGMENTS

I am grateful to so many people who have helped with the creation of this project and the entire Brady Hawk series. Morocco is one of my favorite places I've ever visited and loved setting some scenes in the book there.

Krystal Wade has been a fantastic help in handling the editing of this book, and Dwight Kuhlman has produced another great audio version for your listening pleasure.

I would also like to thank my advance reader team for all their input in improving this book along with all the other readers who have enthusiastically embraced the story of Brady Hawk. Stay tuned ... there's more Brady Hawk coming soon.

ABOUT THE AUTHOR

R.J. PATTERSON is an award-winning writer living in southeastern Idaho. He first began his illustrious writing career as a sports journalist, recording his exploits on the soccer fields in England as a young boy. Then when his father told him that people would pay him to watch sports if he would write about what he saw, he went all in. He landed his first writing job at age 15 as a sports writer for a daily newspaper in Orangeburg, S.C. He later attended earned a degree in newspaper journalism from the University of Georgia, where he took a job covering high school sports for the award-winning *Athens Banner-Herald* and *Daily News*.

He later became the sports editor of *The Valdosta Daily Times* before working in the magazine world as an editor and freelance journalist. He has won numerous writing awards, including a national award for his investigative reporting on a sordid tale surrounding an NCAA investigation over the University of Georgia football program.

R.J. enjoys the great outdoors of the Northwest while living there with his wife and three children. He still follows sports closely. He also loves connecting with readers and would love to hear from you. To stay updated about future projects, connect with him over Facebook or on the interwebs at www.RJPbooks.com and sign up for his newsletter to get deals and updates.

Made in the USA
Monee, IL
26 June 2024